CACTUS FRIENDS

A PSYCHEDELIC LOVE STORY

CHARLOTTE K. DUNE

OCEAN FLOWER PRESS

Publisher's Note:

This is a work of fiction. Names, characters, places and incidents either are the product of the author's imagination or are used fictitiously and any resemblance to actual persons, living or dead, events, or locales is entirely coincidental.

ISBN: 978-1-7343089-0-7

Distributed by Ocean Flower Press.

Cover Photography and Design by Kelly Showker

Cover Models: Nathaniel Cinelli and Jeanine Lamounette

To Agah, for holding my hand on this path.
And to Stephane for inspiring this story.

FOREWORD

I wrote **Cactus Friends: A Psychedelic Love Story** after being inspired by an underground group using entheogens and plant medicine to help heal trauma and addiction. While this story is fiction, *wachuma* and *ayahuasca* have helped many people live happier lives.

This book does not condone the use of illegal substances, but I hope this book will raise awareness and contribute to a body of literature advocating for the decriminalization of beneficial psychedelic medicine and entheogenic plants and compounds.

Cactus Friends: A Psychedelic Love Story is the first book in *The Psychedelic Love Series* by Charlotte Dune.

Order **Mushroom Honeymoon**, Book Two in the Psychedelic Love Series, now via CharlotteDune.com/Mushroom-Honeymoon

To support research and the decriminalization of entheogens, please visit MAPS at www.maps.org.

The triumphs of people living with kidney failure also inspired **Cactus Friends.** To help support innovations in kidney health, please visit The American Kidney Fund.

Unstrap your journey from time.
Find yourself in place.

- Anonymous

1

Thelma never went this far south in Florida. It felt like the dead end of America. Slowing her car to a crawl, she pulled off the narrow, dusty gravel road, and parked in the grass by a rotting wood fence. Tall palm trees and dense brush pressed against the property's perimeter. *Is this the right place?* She double checked her phone. It said she had reached her destination.

Is this a mistake?

Pushing her blonde hair behind her ears, she looked in the rearview mirror, into the end of the afternoon. A field of banana trees flanked the other side of the dirt road, their fronds deep green in the early dusk. The daylight mattered to Thelma. She noticed its quality and divided it into categories, like too-dark, too-bright, flat, florescent, moving shadows, hard-contrast, or purple. Flat was her favorite. She lived for the soft, gray light of a cloudy day, a winter sky without snow, to see every pore on a person's face, but this was not that. The sun rested eye-level to the land. Its fading light leaked between thin clouds, smoldering amber and pink. If she pointed her camera at the horizon, the trees would wear an orange crown. The golden hour glowed, a natural magic.

I could leave now. No one would know.

With her hand, Thelma smoothed the wrinkles out of her lavender gypsy skirt. She never wore this type of hippy-dippy clothing, but the shaman's assistant, Maria, had told her to dress in a long, comfortable skirt.

Who have I become? Honestly, who?

Only two other cars were parked on the road, both empty. She glanced at the car's rearview mirror. Her face looked strange without makeup. No matter how much sunblock she put on her skin in the morning, or what cream she rubbed onto her cheeks at night, she could not stop the progression of sunspots and freckles. They laced across her nose and forehead, like sprinkles of dirt.

Thelma took a deep breath.

It will be ok. No one dies doing this.

She opened the car door and stepped onto the grass swale, tightening the skirt's drawstring around her thin waist. The station wagon was a hand-me-down from her mother, a navy-blue Subaru, but it served her well on photo-shoots. Her lights, tripod, camera bag and props fit in the back. Today though, borrowed camping supplies, a yoga mat, two tarps, paper towels, and a folding chair replaced her photography equipment.

Alone on the road, she gathered her courage and faced the gate. A wood sign, hand-painted with the words, *"La Tierra de Deseos,"* hung from rusted wires. Thelma's Spanish was bad. *Tierra,* she thought was earth, but she didn't know what *Deseos* meant. Before she could look up the word on her phone, a young man opened the gate and stepped out.

"Welcome," he said, grinning to reveal perfect, white teeth. He opened his arms.

He wore no shirt, only stonewashed jeans. He was tall and very tan. Thelma thought he must be twenty-five, or twenty-six, a few years younger than her. His short, sandy blond hair glowed in the sunset. A leather pouch dangled from a string around his neck, resting on his bare chest. Thelma moved her gaze up from the pouch to his aqua blue eyes.

"Hi," Thelma said, unsure of what to do next, her arms stiff by her side.

The man walked over and gave her a sweaty hug.

"Here, I'll help you carry your things," he said.

"Oh, okay, thank you." Thelma stepped out of his embrace. Flustered, she opened the back of her car. It had been a long time since she had hugged a man, much less an attractive one with no shirt. Preparation for the ceremony required no sexual contact with anyone and no masturbation for two weeks before and after the event. The shaman's assistant called it, "protecting your *kundalini* energy." Thelma had never realized how much kundalini energy she possessed until she tried to protect it for two weeks. The man's human touch, the smooth skin on his abdomen made her heart race and her neck sweat.

"Your first time?" he asked.

"Uh yes," she said, trying not to look at his navel, or the space below his navel.

"I'm Claude," he said.

"I'm Thelma."

He pulled out her bags from the back of the car, as if they were weightless. "Come on, let's get you to the circle."

Inside the gate, chickens and roosters roamed free along a dirt path. Colorful parrots in cages squawked at the human visitors. Claude turned down a stone walkway lined with ferns and bushes with bell-shaped, violet flowers. They reached a grassy clearing.

A few other people arranged mats and chairs, unfolded blankets, and took out containers of food. In the center of everyone, hundreds of cut and colorful flowers bordered a rock circle filled with firewood and ash. Latina women in long, white skirts with embroidered red and yellow patterns on the hems buzzed around the fire circle. Others placed sheer fabric, crystals, and candles on a folding plastic table.

Claude led her in an arc, past the guests, to a spot on the right side of the circle.

"You only walk clockwise in the circle," he said. "And you must enter and exit from the same point, where we came in. You can put your food in the main house, but I'll give you some time to set up your mat and things here."

He plopped her bag down on the grass, facing a large, weeping fig tree.

"Once you are settled, take the flowers you brought to Maria." He pointed to a dark-skinned woman in her fifties, with long black and grey hair, in a white dress. "Maria will show you the bathrooms," Claude said. "And she will add your flowers to the altar."

He left to greet the other incoming guests, all carrying camping chairs and blankets.

Thelma unrolled her mat on the edge of the circle, by the tree line. There were so many new sights, smells, and sounds to absorb. It was hard to think about herself, or the reason she had come to the ceremony—her *intention*, as the shaman's assistant had called it on the phone.

Her head rumbled with anxious thoughts. *Will the medicine make me throw up? Will I have diarrhea? Will I lose my mind altogether? Should I leave before it's too late?*

The shaman's assistant said that the *wachuma* cactus had

a male energy. They called it "the grandfather medicine," because of its masculine qualities. It grew in tall stalks on the slopes of the Andes mountains in Ecuador and in Peru. The Spanish colonizers renamed wachuma "San Pedro," referring to the story of Jesus and San Pedro, or Saint Peter in English. In the New Testament of the Bible, Jesus gives Saint Peter the keys to the gates of heaven. The Spanish who tried the wachuma cactus believed it also contained the key to accessing heaven.

"Pretend you are talking to your grandfather," the shaman's assistant had told Thelma on the phone. "Talk to him, tell him your intention, ask him questions. You can even write him a letter before you come."

After much thought and reading and watching as many YouTube videos as she could about San Pedro, and the other hallucinogenic cacti, like Peruvian torch and peyote, Thelma had decided to ask grandfather for something simple, and easy to remember.

"Grandfather, show me my true path."

She had whispered these words, on her knees, next to her living room coffee table, palms pressed together in front of her heart. Of course, as soon as she'd uttered the sentence, Thelma felt foolish, in her condo in Fort Lauderdale, giving an imaginary grandpa commands.

Am I so desperate to figure out my life that I'm talking to made-up plant spirits?

Still, as darkness settled over the farm, she repeated her intention under her breath.

"Grandpa, show me my true path."

"Grandpa, show me my true path."

"Grandpa, show me my true path."

The temperature cooled. Thelma slipped on a burgundy, fleece jacket. It was cold for November, even with the fire burning. She stretched her long legs out on the mat, wearing sneakers with the skirt, to avoid tripping or stubbing her toe in the dark. She always found it uncomfortable to sit on the ground, given her height and her lanky body, less like a model's figure and more like a basketball player's. She stood a foot above most of the men at the ceremony. Many guests filled the clearing now; she estimated forty or fifty people. It was tough for latecomers to find a spot. Claude and Maria came around asking everyone to push back and rearrange things to make room. Her neighbor's blanket was only an inch away.

Children as young as eight or nine years old relaxed in the grass with their parents. Women and men in their late sixties and seventies chatted with each other in Spanish in small groups. To her left sat an older French woman with short brown hair, and on her right, a nervous man from Argentina. She exchanged pleasantries with both her neighbors but tried to avoid further conversation. The man kept looking at Thelma. She dodged his eyes, feeling uncomfortable with the closeness of his mat. She did not want to be unfriendly, but she wanted to concentrate on her intention.

Claude fed air to the fire with a bundle of palm fronds tied together to form a fan.

In the red glimmer of the flames, Maria came forward. "Taita Diego will now open this ceremony."

Taita Diego, the shaman, glowed in the firelight. An older Ecuadorian man, he wore a white canvas, full-length vest with fist-sized flowers in crimson and orange. From his neck hung a beaded necklace with a picture of Jesus Christ in the center, as large as a dinner plate, surrounded by rainbow beads stitched into geometric designs. Embroidered blue-and-yellow parrots flew on the wings of his long robe, draping down his back legs.

Taita Diego faced the sky, palms open and upward. He offered the Lord's Prayer.

"Thy kingdom come, thy will be done."

Thelma mouthed the words of the prayer under her breath, feeling comforted by the familiar tome. It reminded her of praying before bed, at her grandmother's house, on many weekend sleepovers with her cousins. Her grandmother made the kids recite the Lord's Prayer before she tucked everyone in and kissed them goodnight.

Taita Diego finished the prayer and switched to Spanish, with Maria translating, but Thelma was too far from Maria. She strained to listen but could not hear the English words.

Thelma's mind wandered to her friend Camilla.

Although Camilla is not truly my friend, she thought.

Camilla was a yoga teacher she knew. At a baby shower a month before, Thelma had arrived early to take photos. She found Camilla there too, arranging balloons and flowers around the tables, looking younger and stronger than Thelma remembered. *Wow*, she thought, *I really need to do yoga.*

After hugging and saying hello, Thelma had added, "By the way, you look amazing."

Camilla smiled and winked. "I've been experimenting with different plant medicines."

At Thelma's puzzled reaction, Camilla explained that in addition to doing yoga, she drank ayahuasca, mushroom, and San Pedro tea every couple of months in a ceremonial setting.

Thelma wanted to roll her eyes, a yoga teacher taking magical plants sounded so cliché, but something made her stop. Camilla radiated happiness. Her long black hair shone like polished onyx. She floated, buoyant and carefree, full of *joie de vivre*, though Camilla was well into her fifties. While

Thelma felt weighted down and dull, stiff and tired every morning, consumed with worry and indecision. Despite her young age, Thelma's back ached from carrying camera equipment, then hunching over her computer, retouching photos for hours.

As Camilla set flower arrangements on the baby shower tables, she said, "I'll give you the contact for the ceremonies. You should attend one. Maybe start with the San Pedro— that's good for your first time."

"What is San Pedro?" Thelma asked.

"It's a cactus," Camilla said, "but a cactus full of wisdom, like it grew just for humans, to show us our inner worlds."

Thelma took photos, and with every click of her camera, Camilla was there, smiling in each picture, beaming with a force that no one else in the room contained.

After the event, Camilla found her in the parking lot.

"You should go to the ceremony," Camilla said. "It will be an unforgettable experience. Many find that the ceremonies add meaning to their creative work." She motioned to Thelma's camera bag.

Thelma looked at her camera. A hollow, empty feeling caught in her throat. Whether it was early morning fatigue, lack of sleep, or something deeper, tears rose in her eyes. She did want her art to have more meaning. It had no value to her now besides income. Her photos even stressed out her clients. Most hired her to appease some egotistical, social media instinct or obligation, to aggrandize themselves to their peers. When they saw the photos, regardless of Thelma's heavy retouching, the reality of their appearances never met their expectations. Rarely were people content with their own image. Their faces fell. On the exterior, they praised the pictures, but disappointment emanated from their interiors.

During art school, she had imagined her work hanging on gallery walls, challenging perceptions and exploring controversial topics, but any creative spark she possessed then was lost now in the deluge of Instagram hashtags and Pinterest posts that she used to promote her business. The incessant pressure to bring in more clients by turning her photos into advertisements dulled her artistic instincts. She had run out of new ideas.

Clenching her jaw, she turned away from Camilla. A tear slid onto her cheek, and she immediately wiped it away in a motion designed to look like she was just rubbing her eyes. She would not tear-up in front of this yoga-goddess's patronizing calm. Shutting the back of her car, equipment all packed up, Thelma inhaled through her nose and faced Camilla, who stood still, staring at her with a hawk's focus.

"Okay," Thelma heard herself say, "do they have a website?" Hot and tired, she wanted to get in the air-conditioned car and away from Camilla's piercing gaze.

Camilla laughed, "This isn't something you Google, my dear. Give me your number and I'll text you the details. But brace yourself," she continued, "For the rapé. They do rapé at each ceremony. It's like snuff, but blown up your nose, but it's fine, intense, but good."

Blown up your nose? That sounded disgusting.

Still, when the contact came through the next day, Thelma, remembering Camilla's permanent smile and dancing, vibrant eyes, made the call.

Working their way around the circle, Claude and Taita Diego passed out the rapé. Thelma craned her neck and squinted, but she could not see what each person received.

She waited, anxious. She tried to focus on her breath, but her heart drummed faster and faster in her chest. The two men finally came to face her. Claude cradled a pouch of wet tobacco. She looked up at him, his handsome frame silhouetted dark in front of the bonfire. He poured the pulp and tobacco juice into Thelma's hand. She stared at the black liquid in her palm.

No one dies from this.

As she'd watched the French woman next to her do first, she snorted the rapé out of her palm like a line of cocaine, if the cocaine was a cupful of dirty water.

The instant the rapé hit her nose, it burned with the intensity of a poblano pepper. Her face rushed with heat and tears welled from her eyes. A sneeze threatened to force its way out, but she held her breath, trying to hold in the medicine. Maria handed her a small plastic bag that they called a 'wellness bag,' but which was actually the kind of bag people used to pick up dog poop. The rapé tasted like tobacco and stung as it trickled down the back of her throat. The shaman instructed her to spit it out, rather than swallowing the acrid liquid.

Others threw up and vomited into their bags. The retching sounds made Thelma want to heave, but within five minutes the burning went away. Wide-awake and ready, she looked up at the stars now filling the night sky.

Grandfather, show me my path.

The red fire danced with flames. Taita Diego returned to the top of the circle. With the help of Claude and Maria, he distributed the San Pedro. Thelma realized she would be one of the last people to receive the medicine, because of where she was sitting.

While Claude administered the San Pedro, the shaman shook a rattle and blew from his tobacco pipe onto each person, circulating smoke around their bodies, waving a fan of brown and white feathers.

Thelma felt like a cultural vampire, partaking in this ancient ritual, but unable to understand the words spoken. Still, Maria had told her on the phone that they welcomed Westerners to the ceremonies.

"It's not cultural appropriation," Maria had said. "This belongs to all of us on Earth. We don't own this plant or the idea of this medicine. Our ancestors discovered it and we want to share it with as many people as we can reach, because these ceremonies have the power to save the world and protect our lands if people can understand."

When Thelma's turn came, Claude reached into a mason jar, filled with what looked like clumps of green dirt. He scooped out the concoction and formed it into a ball. It was the San Pedro cactus ground up and mixed with water. He placed the ball in Thelma's hand. Crumblier than cookie dough, it had a gritty texture, like wet sand.

Thelma took a deep breath, opened her lips, and popped in the ball. As soon as she started to chew it, the San Pedro de-particularized and went to every corner of her mouth, between her teeth and under her tongue. She gagged. It tasted metallic, like blood mixed with grass, a rusty pipe; she reached for the right words in her mind to describe the putrid, unbearable taste.

I'm poisoning myself, she thought.

Her eyes watered. She sputtered and drooled. Losing her inhibitions, she scraped around in her mouth with her finger, to remove the remaining cactus from her gums.

"It's ok," Claude whispered, kneeling in front of her. He touched her shoulder. "Drink this, it will help. It's the San Pedro tea."

He poured her a small glass of what looked like apple

juice. She gulped the tea, trying to wash away the grit of the cactus, but it tasted almost as bad as the paste. Thelma gasped and swallowed the rest of the liquid. Squeezing her lips together, she struggled not to vomit.

"Now, no more water till the end of the ceremony when we give the go-ahead," Claude said.

The shaman blew smoke around her body and waved his feathers. The pair moved on.

Thelma felt nothing unusual, aside from the terrible rusty taste in her mouth. About twenty minutes passed. The adrenaline rush from swallowing the San Pedro dissipated. She tried to relax. Beside her, the Argentinian man hunched over, clutching his wellness bag to his face.

She leaned closer to him. "Are you ok?"

The man shook his head and gripped the bag, his arm muscles tense. He spasmed and vomited. Thelma pulled out a roll of paper towel and tore him off a piece to wipe his mouth. She patted his back. She rarely touched strangers, much less strange men, but it seemed like the right thing to do. Her hand looked gigantic on his t-shirt in the moonlight.

The better to hold my camera with, she thought.

In school, the boys had called her *Thelma-man-hands*; she had forgotten about that.

"Thank you," the man murmured. "Thank you."

"You'll be fine soon," she said, with a calm confidence that came from nowhere she knew.

He continued to empty the contents of his stomach into his wellness bag.

He needs a new bag. She laughed to herself. *We all need a new bag sometimes.*

Thelma handed him an extra plastic bag she had brought in case her clothes got soiled and she needed to change. As he took the bag from her hand, she noticed that his hands were very small. *He has baby fingers,* she thought. She squinted, trying to see his fingers better. It was true. He had six baby fingers. She stared. *Six?* She counted them again. Six fingers. No, he had truncated, knuckle-length stubs. She blinked. *Am I hallucinating?*

A wave of heat rushed up inside her like fire burning bones.

Here we go, Thelma thought. *There's no turning back now.*

Moving in three-dimensional space, on their Z-axis, the stars curled closer to Earth. The fig tree bent down and transformed into a spirit animal. Claude and the shaman danced around the fire.

They look like Mexican kachina dolls, Thelma thought. This mental image multiplied and vibrated. She laughed at the doll-men, carrying their feathers and shaking their rattles like bopping children's toys. Faces breathed in the tree's branches. Illustrations of skeletons danced in black-and-white masks. Like jovial court jesters, they did not scare her.

Her stomach churned. She 'got well' three of four times, but the nausea persisted. Forgetting her intention, she watched the constellations overhead and the shadows on the trees, consumed by the simple passing of time. Shooting stars streaked the sky, streaming horizontal trails of glowing dust behind them, slow-motion silver airplanes.

The energy of the shaman, of Claude, and of Maria impressed her. After eating and drinking the sacred cactus, they continued to dance with vigor, to sing and chant, to play drums and rattles, to tend the fire, help the sick, and show people to the bathrooms.

As the hours passed, her visions changed. The dolls shifted shapes to waves of light, the spines of the San Pedro plant, oscillating fibers, green luminous seaweed swaying in black sand when she closed her eyes. Finally, the nausea subsided. She returned to her intention.

> *Grandfathershowmemypath*
> *Grandfathershowmemypath*
> *Grandfathershowmemypath.*

Holding the phrase in a circle, like the rocks around the fire, she connected one word to the next.

Shadows created shapes on the leaves and trunk of the fig tree. In the bark, letters formed from a luminescent liquid-gold.

SIMON

What?

Grandfather, what?

SIMON

The name whispered to her, a sound radiation, a painting in lights.

Her eyes widened. She did know a *Simon*.

She shook her head. *No. GrandfatherShowMeMyPath-GranfatherShowMeMyPath.*

The command turned urgent.

The letters remained.

SIMON

GRANDFATHERSHOWMEMYPATH.

SIMON

Thelma spoke silently, *But why grandfather? What does Simon mean?*

SIMON

The tree issued no other response.

But how is that my path? Should I call the real Simon?

WHAT ABOUT SIMON?

The name disappeared. The moon crossed left to right in its cosmic dome. Night faded to indigo and then to the pale cool of a blue jay's feather. Planes flew overhead to the Miami airport. The sun warmed the air. Claude passed around cups of water for everyone.

Thelma gulped the water, racked with an intense thirst. She moved from her mat to her camping chair, leaned back, and cried. Long, wet tears fell to her lap, absorbing into the fabric of her purple skirt.

The Argentinian man next to her asked, "Are you okay?"

She nodded, pulling the blanket to her face, still crying.

Simon. Why?

She needed a clear answer, but grandfather granted only a mystery to unravel.

Thelma pictured Simon, his beach house, a lazy Sunday, so many years ago. The San Pedro took her to a memory so real that she could explore it deeper than the first time. She viewed it from every angle, at every moment, as her, as Simon, as the sea outside his window. She smelled him, his olive skin. She touched the small scar on his forehead. He laughed in baritone bellows, reminding her not to take life so seriously. On the weekends, they drank vodka martinis and watched old movies in black and white, like *Casablanca* and *Cat on a Hot Tin Roof*. He cooked enormous, gut-busting Italian lunches, serving her homemade gnocchi, pouring cream sauce over her plate. After eating, they snuggled on his sofa, under a bottom bedsheet, sticking their toes in the elastic edge, covering themselves like mummies. When he tickled her, she giggled and screamed for him to stop.

But why Simon? Why now?

Thelma cried until the shaman came. Drinking from a tiny bottle, he spat cool, blue liquid onto her face in a fine mist.

Her trance broke.

"What was that?" she asked the French woman beside her. "It smells minty."

"Florida Water," the woman said. "It closes the ceremony and cleanses you."

Thelma wiped the tears and the Florida Water off her face and focused her attention on the new, golden morning.

Real life resumed. She needed to pee. Standing up, shaky and disoriented, Thelma went clockwise around the circle, to the path leading to the farm's bathroom. Birdcages and fruit trees covered the property. Potted plants surrounded a tiki hut, with an open-air kitchen and a seating area that offered a place to decompress after the ceremony. A few women sat on the sofas, looking dazed and sick. Four men leaned against the bar, drinking coconut water and making small talk. Thelma's need to use the toilet grew more pressing. She headed into the wooden bathroom stalls. Relieved that there was no line for the toilet, she released her stomach. Roosters drowned out the sound of her bowels emptying what felt like pounds of intestinal matter.

She emerged from the bathroom, renewed, and washed her hands in a small, outdoor sink. As she walked back to the group, she could not stop thinking about Simon. *Why had grandfather wachuma presented that vision?* Deep in thought, she bumped into a man.

Thelma lost her balance and stumbled. Catching herself, she leaned sideways in an awkward tilt.

"You okay there?" the man asked.

She forced a smile. "I think I'm still feeling the medicine more than I realize."

"I saw you crying at the end of the ceremony— it looked like you were having a bit of a rough time." He cocked his head and eyed her.

Thelma steadied herself. "It wasn't too bad. More tears of joy than tears of sadness."

Their eyes met.

He was older than her. Long black hair fell in waves halfway down his back. Lean and tall, he wore a gray, long-sleeve t-shirt, blue jeans, and leather sandals. A five o'clock shadow, tan skin, and dark eyes gave him a gritty appeal.

He stuck out his hand, "I'm Saman."

"I'm Thelma," she said, shaking his hand.

He stared at her, as if trying to decide what else to say.

"Well, I'll let you get to the bathroom," she said.

"Nice to meet you."

"You too." She smiled and walked back to the circle.

. . .

MARIA LAY out Hawaiian sweet bread, watermelon, and juicy slices of star fruit. The shaman blessed the offering, and people surrounded the food and repeated the Lord's Prayer. They ate and chatted, excited, laughing, but Thelma wanted to hide under her blanket and sob.

Saman walked over to her chair.

"Hey," he said.

"Hey."

"You're not hungry?"

"Not really," Thelma replied.

"Me neither, I don't think my stomach is ready."

He sat in the grass beside her chair and stretched his long, angular, tan legs out in front of him, crossing his ankles, leaning back on his palms.

He looked up at Thelma. "Have you been to one of these before?"

"No, this is my first time. Have you?"

"No."

"Did you see anything?" Thelma asked, too tired to consider if her question was appropriate or impolite.

He raised his eyebrows. "Oh I saw some stuff. Not what I was expecting though."

"What did you see?"

Saman gazed at the ashes from the fire. "I was a bird. I mean, not an actual bird, but dressed up as one, with yellow and blue feathers attached to me, like a Native American dancer or something, and I was sitting by a river." He paused to see if she was bored.

"Are you Native?" She asked.

"Me? No. I'm not like Seminole or anything."

"Where are you from?"

"Uh Pembroke Pines." He grinned. "But you mean originally? My family is from Iran. I'm Persian."

"Oh wow," Thelma said. "I mean that's stupid I guess to say 'oh wow,' but I wasn't expecting that answer. I thought you were Indian, maybe."

He laughed. "I get that a lot."

"What happened next? You just sat by the river?" She wanted to ask him what his intention was for the ceremony but decided it was too private a question to ask a stranger.

"No, so then I'm in the feathers and I got in the river and I waded out and then I realized the feathers were coming off and floating away. I tried to gather them all up, but the water was moving too fast. I could only grab a few." He paused and closed his eyes, remembering the vision. "And then it ended, that was it."

"That sounds beautiful, though," Thelma said, not knowing how to respond.

"Yeah," he said, "it was."

He did not sound convinced. Thelma sensed a sadness inside him, like a secret.

"What about you?" Saman asked.

Thelma fidgeted with a string coming out from the seam in her skirt. "It was weird," she said. "I didn't see much. I just saw like a name."

"A name? Like written out?"

"Yeah, like letters, like a sign in gold letters." She frowned. "So random."

"What was the name?"

She looked at the fig tree. "The name of someone I used to know."

"Are they still alive?"

"I guess. We lost touch. I hadn't thought about them in years."

She did not say it was Simon. She was playing the pronoun game, embarrassed to tell Saman that it was a man's name. With this realization, she understood that she was attracted to Saman.

"Hmm," he said, as if reading her thoughts. "You should get in touch with them. These plants open us to things we otherwise can't perceive. It's definitely trying to tell you something."

"Maybe. I haven't talked to them in over a decade."

She squinted. It was ten or eleven o'clock, but she was nowhere near sober enough to drive back home. Why hadn't she brought sunglasses?

"What do you think your vision means?" she asked Saman.

"I don't know. Maybe I'm worried about losing a part of myself that I can't get back, like the feathers floating away."

"Or maybe you are losing them because you don't need them?"

"That's a much better interpretation." He flashed a smile at her.

They lapsed into silence. The other guests packed up their chairs and bags and started to leave. She did not want the encounter with Saman to end. Claude rolled out a wool blanket and arranged leather pouches, feather fans, and beaded necklaces on it to sell to the people leaving. He selected a few pieces of jewelry and worked his way around the crowd.

Reaching Saman and Thelma, he pulled out two bracelets.

"Here you go," Claude said. "To commemorate your first plant medicine ceremony."

One bracelet was red and black with beads, and the other was blue, yellow, white, and gold.

"Twenty dollars each," Claude said.

Thelma smiled. "They are beautiful. Did you make them?"

"Of course." Claude took Thelma's hand and slipped the blue and yellow one onto her wrist. "There you go, fits you perfectly."

Thelma admired the bracelet. "I would, but I don't have cash with me."

Saman leaned in. "Here, here, we will get both."

"Oh, you don't need to do that." Thelma blushed.

"Nonsense," said Claude, "let the handsome man buy you a bracelet." He winked at Saman and took the forty dollars.

"Now you'll never forget your first ceremony." Claude grinned.

"As if we ever would," Saman said.

"Oh, my gosh, it's beautiful, but here Saman, you take the blue and yellow one, it matches your vision, and I'll take the black and red one."

"You're right. Good call."

They switched bracelets.

"Now what?" he said. "Are you going back to Miami?"

"No." Thelma looked at the bracelet; the pattern was that of a repeating sun in red on the black beads. "I have to drive all the way to Fort Lauderdale."

"Oh, awesome, I live in Fort Lauderdale too."

"Really? Wow, I assumed everyone lived closer."

"Me too." Saman smiled.

Neither of them moved to get up to leave. Maria and Claude packed up the ceremony, while the shaman sat under a tree, fanning and talking to an older woman who was still in a trance.

To keep the conversation going, Thelma blurted, "Hey, I'm a photographer."

"Really? That's awesome."

"Yeah, I, um, this might sound strange, but maybe I could photograph you reenacting your vision? If you wanted?" The idea developed in an instant in her mind and became a finished image. "I've got feathers from shooting newborns, and we could go to a canal or river." They would go late in the afternoon. Saman would wade in the water shirtless. The final pictures would be stunning. "I'll make it fun, I promise," she heard herself say.

He hesitated. "I don't know, I'm not great at smiling for cameras and stuff. I don't even have an Instagram account."

"You don't have to smile. I know it's weird. It was just an idea." She backpedaled. *Why must I be so socially awkward*?

He touched her arm. "No, it's really nice of you. Let's do it. Make it a trade—the bracelet for the photo."

"Perfect," she said, her heart pounding.

"But on one condition," Saman said.

"What condition?"

"You contact the person whose name you saw and give me a full report on what happens."

She recoiled, eyes wide. *How would she even find Simon? What would she say?*

THE LONG DRIVE back to Fort Lauderdale was grueling; Thelma's body ached in the driver's seat, stiff from sitting and lying on the ground. Fields of palm trees and pineapple farms stood in lines, tropical totems on an otherworldly plane. The car floated on the pavement. *This isn't normal. I'm still tripping. God help me get home in one piece*, Thelma thought. Black crows flew across the road. Cars and trucks rushed past her on the Florida Turnpike. She wanted to stop to buy a drink at a gas station but worried that she looked too high. The names Simon and Saman bobbed and weaved in her thoughts, two kachina dolls dancing in the tree.

Rubbing her eyes, she gritted her teeth and gripped the steering wheel like the safety bar on a roller coaster, willing herself home.

3

Thelma hunched in front of her computer, pondering which keys to push. She typed 'Simon' into the Google search field, but something stopped her from entering his last name. She fluttered her fingertips on the keyboard, playing a fake piano, not hard enough to hit a letter.

Just type it, she thought. But she couldn't.

The Intracoastal Waterway gleamed in the high-noon sun, visible out the window by her desk. She had picked the small condo for the view, for the light, and for the floor-to-ceiling windows that created the perfect soft-box of sun. Her mother had told her she was an idiot for paying so much rent for the tiny place.

"I want to see the ocean every day," she'd replied.

"The Intracoastal is not the ocean. It's a river," her mother had said.

"It's saltwater, isn't it? Close enough."

Was it saltwater? She didn't even know. She deleted 'Simon' from the search bar and typed in 'Intracoastal Waterway.'

"*Natural inlets, saltwater rivers, bays, sounds, and canals create a 3,000-mile transportation route parallel to the Atlantic Ocean.*"

Maybe I can shoot Saman on one of the smaller offshoots of the Intracoastal, she thought, in an area with a lot of foliage.

To photograph him in a river might be risky, because alligators frequented freshwater, but they would not go into the canals near the ocean because of the brackish, salty water.

The only problem was that canals could be very dirty. I can't ask him to get in a canal, she thought. Why did I commit to this? He probably won't even call.

Is this just a stupid idea?

Picking up her cell, she checked to see if anyone had sent a text message. No one had. She kept her phone on silent 24/7, a habit she'd learned from a podcast for creative artists. She tried to only look at the phone if she felt the urge to, not if someone else wanted her to, avoiding absent-minded scrolling.

She read her last message to Saman, sent five days ago:

— *Hi- this is Thelma, from the ceremony.*

— *Thanks! This is Saman from the ceremony :-)*

She didn't want to say more. He had her number. If he didn't call, they wouldn't do the shoot.

Thirsty, she went to the kitchen and opened the fridge. There wasn't much—a few Diet Lightning Sharks, a can of sparkling water, almond milk, leftover kale salad, a bag of apples, some baby carrots, and a bunch of old condiments like ginger-soy-apricot dressing that she never used.

Thelma eyed the Diet Lightning Shark. Maria had warned her off caffeine until two weeks after the ceremony.

"Let your brain sit with the San Pedro," Maria had said, "before you introduce another compound. Caffeine is a plant master, just like nicotine, alcohol, or marijuana. It is best to wait."

Thelma wasn't a big drinker—an occasional glass of chardonnay or champagne at a party, never beer, and maybe a cosmopolitan on the rare occasion that she went out to a nightclub or bar—but she loved Diet Lightning Sharks. Though her mother was ruining this simple pleasure. After reading an article that cited Diet Lightning Sharks as causing dementia, her mother referred to them as 'D-Sharks,' with the D for dementia.

"Are you still drinking D-Sharks?" her mom would ask her on the phone.

"No," Thelma would lie.

She scowled, pulled out the can of sparkling water and an apple, and returned to her desk.

Not that Simon would be hard to find. On the contrary, he would be too easy to find. As soon as she finished typing in his name, his image would appear on the screen. She would see where he was working and his latest journal articles. Once found, the decision would face her—contact him, or ignore the vision?

Restless, she gulped the soda water. She chomped the apple down to the core and threw it hard into the trashcan, hitting the bottom with a clang.

Sometimes she felt like a tortured artist, tossed about by her own ideas and rustling thoughts. Her creative visions rose like yeast in bread, then fell flat. She questioned everything. Could she ever get anything meaningful done? Of all her amazing concepts, for photo shoots or art videos, for collages, self-portraits, or gallery installations, none came to fruition. She forgot them as time passed, rubbed out of her mind like the zits she Photoshopped off brides.

Ugh. She shook her head. *Concentrate on one thing,* she reminded herself. *Just finish one thing.*

With her half-finished soda water, she opened Instagram on her phone, and searched for images tagged #Intracoastal, #FortLauderdale.

There are no new ideas, she thought. Someone probably already has done the same photoshoot you want to do.

Sure enough, near the top of the search results was a picture of a tan, pregnant woman with blond hair, standing in a river wearing a flimsy, white, string bikini. Trees and shrubs surrounded her, without a building in sight.

Bingo.

The photo tags read #maternity #Intracoastal #Fort-Lauderdale #museum #gardens #BonnetHouseMuseumandGardens.

She had been to the Bonnet House Museum and Gardens on a failed Tinder date. The old mansion straddled a rivulet running off the Intracoastal. The property had belonged to the poet-daughter of a wealthy New England merchant. After her death, the family donated it to the city to become a historical site. They charged a photography fee, but it was small, $25, well worth a good shoot, with no boats or crowds of people.

She checked the clock on her phone. Only three hours remained before she needed to be at a charity event to take photos. Not enough time to go to the gardens, look around, get back, and be ready.

She opened another browser tab.

Simon.

Out of the corner of her eye, her phone's screen lit up.

Someone was calling. She grabbed the phone and read the caller's name.

Saman From Cactus Ceremony.

Adrenalin rushed through her. *Should I answer? Or let it go to voice mail?*

She answered.

"Hello."

"Hey, this is Saman from the ceremony the other day."

"Oh hey, how are you?" she said fast, breathless.

God, why can't I just talk like a normal person?

"I'm good, just seeing if you still wanted to get together and do this photoshoot?"

"Yeah, let's do it," she said. "I mean, if you still want to?" Her heart pounded.

"Yeah, for sure."

"You can come to my apartment first, and then we can go to the location together."

He hesitated.

"I mean, is that weird? I'm thinking it is better to go in one car, because we might have to pay for parking."

"Okay, I mean, good with me if it's good with you."

His voice was silky; an image of his smooth, muscular shoulders came to Thelma. She imagined rubbing sunblock on his back.

"Yes. I'll see you next Saturday? If you come around three we can set up and get out there before dark."

"Okay, cool."

"Great, I'll see you then." She wanted to wrap up the call and go back to her fantasy, rather than continue the bumbling conversation.

But instead of saying goodbye, Saman said, "So, did you call your friend? What was his name?"

Thelma stumbled on her words. "Simon. Ugh. No, I haven't."

"How come?"

"Um. You know, I don't have his phone number and it seems weird."

"Was he like a boyfriend or something?" Saman asked.

Thelma's shoulders tightened, her neck muscles tensed. She closed her eyes. There was Simon, laughing, hugging her, tickling her under the covers.

"He was a mentor," she half-lied, "that I had when I was younger. I really admired him."

Why am I omitting the truth?

"Another photographer?"

"No, more of a philosopher. He taught media studies."

"Oh, so like a professor you had."

She hesitated. Simon was a professor, but not one that she had ever had, at least not in the classroom.

"Yep," she lied.

"Yeah, I guess that is weird—a beautiful young student calling him years later," Saman said.

A smile broke across Thelma's face. *Beautiful and young?*

"Flattery will get you everywhere," she said.

He laughed.

"Okay, well," she said, "so I'll see you next Saturday."

"Regardless, I think you should email Simon," Saman repeated. "These plants are the jungle's television; they broadcast the news of your subconscious."

SHE HUNG UP, got off her chair, and slumped onto the sofa, closing her eyes. She had not masturbated for three weeks.

Perhaps I'm so distracted because I haven't had an orgasm, she thought with disdain, ready to explode.

She Googled for the fourth time, "Sex and San Pedro side effects" but nothing came up except for a few new-age sites advising San Pedro experiences. She sighed and slipped off her jeans, leaving them in a crumple on the floor.

Thelma set her phone alarm for two hours, lay down on the couch, and closed her eyes. As she imagined rubbing Saman's bare chest with sunblock on the beach, sweat warmed between her thighs. *Jungle television? Don't those cacti grow in the desert?* Before she could consider this question further, sleep whisked her away.

IN THE LIQUID darkness of her dream, Thelma entered a dim hospital room. A man with black hair lay in a bed. The space smelled of formaldehyde and rubbing alcohol. A heart monitor beeped and a respirator breathed air in and out, via a mask and tube obscuring the man's face. Daylight shone in through an open window on the back wall.

Strange sounds emanated from outside, shrieking and flapping noises.

Someone whispered, "*Thelma.*"

The man in bed slept. An IV ran up his arm.

She realized—the man was Simon.

"Simon!" Thelma raced to his side and grabbed his limp hand. "Simon, wake up, it's me, Thelma." She nudged his arm. "Simon, wake up."

She stared at him in disbelief. His tan skin was smooth, his eyes closed, his black hair cut short. He looked at peace. Only his glasses were missing.

"Simon!" She shook his arm, harder this time, but he did not wake up.

Fear gripped her. *What was happening?* She had a

horrible sense of foreboding. "Simon, wake up," she whispered.

Simon did not move.

The shrieking outside intensified. She let go of Simon's hand and followed the sound to the window.

A vast, light green meadow of grass extended to the horizon, blades waving in the sun like a carpet tossed into the sea. She was high up, on the fifteenth or twentieth floor of the hospital.

"Thelma," a man's voice called.

She looked down. Below the window, a man shouted, "Thelma, look up."

A black cloud floated overhead. No, it was a circle of birds, not an open ring, but a solid sphere of black birds. *Were they vultures?* They crowed together and beat their wings.

Dread overwhelmed her. The person shouting on the ground was Saman.

She jerked her head inside the hospital room. Simon's heart monitor beeped wildly, his pulse crashing. Hundreds of vultures shrieked like pigs.

As she bolted out of sleep, Thelma grabbed her phone to shut off her alarm. Sweat trickled from her armpits and under her breasts. She wrapped her arms around herself, rocking back and forth on the couch. The dream was so real. *What the fuck just happened? How long have I been asleep?*

Not bothering to pull on her jeans, she plopped onto her computer chair in her tank-top and underwear and opened Facebook. She typed in the two words she'd been avoiding all day.

'Simon Amalfitano.'

And there he was, as she remembered him, stocky, but not fat, with thick arms and a short torso, wearing khaki pants and a navy-blue sport coat with a white button-down shirt. He stood outside on a green lawn with a young woman holding a diploma. Was she his daughter, now all grown up, with curly black hair and a bright smile? The caption of the photo read, "Never a prouder father there was."

Thelma scrolled down through the photos that would show on his page without them being connected as friends. There were sunrises and snowy streets, some scientific articles, but no more images of Simon or of his wife.

She remembered the morning his wife had called her cellphone. In a hotel room, their naked bodies knotted together like challah bread, Simon was running his fingers through her hair when the phone rang. She had reached for it on the hotel's nightstand. It was Simon's home number. Time froze.

"Should I answer?" she asked him, heart pounding.

"Answer but deny," Simon whispered.

His wife's voice was breathy and sad. "Please," his wife had said, "leave our family alone."

But they hadn't, they couldn't. They hid, they made love; they saved each other in their phones under fake names. They sent cryptic, childish messages, like, *I need to study my French. Can you meet me and bring your pen?*

To suspect her father's colleague was her lover was so unlikely and shocking that it was unfathomable. They sat next to each other at dinners with her parents and the other professors; no one ever guessed.

Until two years into the affair, when Simon's wife discovered their emails.

Her parents had never been so disappointed in her.

Simon resigned and took a position in New York before the university could fire him. His family needed a fresh start, he said, in a new place. They had to end things.

But even after getting caught, they still found ways to see each other—conferences, trips, daytime trysts.

It wasn't until Thelma decided she wanted more than a part-time boyfriend that the affair ended. *Ironic,* she thought, *since now I've got no boyfriend at all.*

As she looked at the picture of him with his daughter, emotions swelled in Thelma. She opened the message window, and started to type, but stopped. In a flash of bravery, she tapped the icon to initiate a call.

Somewhere, in New York City, as the sun faded and the evening chill crept in, Simon's phone rang.

4

S aman walked down the parking deck stairs with a
sense of destiny. Then again, *did everything feel like
that lately*? Since the San Pedro ceremony, he'd cared
less about anything. *Is this the beginning of the end*? he
wondered. Obstacles at work faded from his concern.

As he headed to the building where Thelma lived he
noticed his empty hands. He only carried his ID, a money
clip, and a credit card stuck into his jean pocket.

Should I have gotten flowers? he considered. *She is doing
me a favor.*

Who was this girl so eager to take his picture? He might
have canceled, but it seemed rude when she had been so
sweet at the ceremony. *It is probably me doing her a favor,* he
decided. He had concluded recently that every action
everyone did was transactional and selfish. *So why am I
doing her the favor*? That was the real question. *Why am I
here*? He supposed he wanted to see her photo of his vision.
But why? Or am I just a pussy who can't say no? Maybe it was a
desire to capture himself looking strong, one last time
before fate made a final turn and changed him into a weak,

decrepit man. That was it. *How sad,* he thought, *and I don't even have the balls or the goddam decency to tell her the truth.*

Sweating, in a long black t-shirt, he entered the tall condo building. He wasn't ready to show his arms, not to this girl. Not to anyone. Things were worse now. They got worse every week.

Polished, white marble floors fed into a grandiose lobby with high ceilings and a concierge's desk. This wasn't what Saman was expecting from the outdoorsy-looking young woman he'd met at the cactus ceremony. *How much would this place rent for?* Surely for more than his cement condo, near Fort Lauderdale's many halfway-houses and rows of rehabs.

Saman's neighborhood was concrete lawns and rows of cracker-box houses, 1950s homes halved or quartered into multiple-unit apartments. Uneven pavement, potholes, parked cars, kid's bicycles, empty beer cans, cigarette butts, and abandoned needles covered his street. Visitors locked their car doors when they drove by.

Did she have a day job? He couldn't remember. Or rich parents? *Must be nice,* he thought.

The concierge buzzed him onto the elevator.

As he pressed the button to go up to Thelma's floor, anxiety crept into his thoughts. What if she wanted him to take off his shirt? He just wouldn't. Or maybe he would strip it off and watch her reaction. Deliberate awkwardness was sometimes the best way to control situations.

He paused at Thelma's apartment, but before he could ring her bell, she opened the door. He stepped back, surprised.

"Hey, I saw you on the doorbell camera," she smiled.

The peephole wasn't a hole; it was a camera.

Stupid me, he thought.

Thelma glowed. Had she put on that self-tanner stuff girls wore? In tight jean shorts and a fitted white tank-top, she was more attractive than he remembered. A yellow bikini top peaked through her shirt. He pulled his gaze up to her face.

"Hey." He leaned in and air-kissed her on one cheek with a light hug. Was this a date? No, it can't be. *I don't date, not anymore.*

"Come in," she said, "This is exciting."

"Yeah, I've never had my picture taken before by a real photographer," Saman said. "I mean not since I was a kid at school."

"That doesn't count." She smiled.

Minimal and modern, somber photographs of the ocean in shades of gray hung in matted frames, giving the apartment a pre-fabricated atmosphere, like it was staged by a realtor.

"Are those your photos?" Saman asked.

"Yeah, I went through an aquatic phase." She looked at the picture above her sofa—de-saturated, grainy waves on a white sky. "Moving on from that now. These are pretty old."

"They're beautiful," Saman said. "They look like something out of a furniture store, very professional."

He meant it as a compliment, but seeing her reaction, he realized he had said the wrong thing.

"Yeah, very commercial," she shrugged. "That's what I seem to be good at is commercial photography."

"That is where the money is, right?" He looked around the apartment.

She changed the subject. "So, let me show you what I've gathered up. I thought you might cancel since this is kind of weird, so I left the tags on everything."

"Oh no, I wouldn't have," he lied. "This is too special."

She smiled. "You are too kind. Okay, I've got everything in my room. Follow me."

Her bedroom had the same austere look of the rest of the apartment, except for three wood shelves laden with camera lenses, chargers, light bulbs, and batteries.

"Wow," he said. "You've got quite a collection."

"Too much stuff." She glanced at the shelves. "I should probably sell half of it."

"And wow, you nailed the colors," Saman said, pointing to her bed. Feathers in royal blue and canary yellow covered her gray duvet.

"I've also got some black ones to create shadows," she said. "I got something called spirit gum to attach them, but then I realized it will be hard to remove, so I think it's better if we use double-stick tape."

They stood next to each other, looking at the feathers on her bed. Saman sensed hot energy radiating from Thelma, but he couldn't tell if it was sexual or artistic.

"How were the feathers in the vision?" she asked. "Sticking up like this? Or hanging down?" She held a down-turned feather to his chest. He stiffened and reflexively sucked in his stomach.

"Let me think about that." He closed his eyes. The image remained vivid in his mind. It was not angel wings; rather, feathers stuck up all over him, like he was a person hiding in feathers.

Saman opened his eyes and caught Thelma staring at him. He locked onto her blue eyes for a moment, before she averted them back to the feather by his arm.

"Up," he said. "The feathers were up."

She rotated the feather. "Like this?"

"Yes."

Side by side, they unwrapped the feathers. A silence

took hold, aside from the rustling of the packaging plastic. She smelled like strawberries, or was it expensive perfume? Or sunblock? They collected the feathers in one tote bag to take to the river.

Saman wondered if he should tell her now, or wait. No words formed on his lips, so he kept silent until all the feathers were in the bag.

"This is a lot of feathers," he said. "Are you sure they're all going to fit on me?"

"I bought a lot because I want this to be spectacular, to do justice to your vision."

Their arms almost touched as they stood by the bed. He wanted to touch her, so he did. He turned to face her and placed his hand on her shoulder.

"Thank you," he said. "This means a lot to me."

She smiled and looked down. "Don't worry, it's as much for me as it is for you. I love creative projects. This is a welcome break from babies and happy couples."

On the word *couples,* she looked up at him and their eyes caught again. Hers were pale-blue, almost green, with long, brown eyelashes. He didn't ask if she had a boyfriend; he could tell she did not. *Maybe I'll kiss her later,* Saman thought. *No. Don't do that, you idiot.*

Instead, he asked, "So, did you call your friend, Simon?"

She stepped back, the spell broken.

"I did actually," she said, "but he didn't answer."

"Good," Saman said. "He will probably call you back."

"Maybe the vision was just for me to think about him as an influence." She took the bag of feathers and went into the living room and Saman followed. "I think he would approve of this photoshoot," she said. "He was always supportive of my art."

"I'm sure whatever is meant to be will be," Saman said.

"If you believe in that. Come on, let's go. We want to time the light right."

Saman wondered about Simon's real identity. Surely, he had been more than a mentor, judging by the look in Thelma's eyes when she said his name.

"Hey, sorry, I didn't mean to be nosey," he apologized. "I'm not great at minding my business."

"Speaking of business," she said, moving her camera bag and tripod by the door. "You never told me what you do."

Saman smiled, "I work for the news. Hence why I'm nosey! I edit other people's business."

"You are a journalist? That is so cool."

"No, I do sound editing for the Sunshine Hello Morning Show, and I edit radio commercials."

"Oh my god, I've totally listened to that show. Wow!"

His job impressed her, as it did most people in South Florida, even though to him it was a shit gig.

"Yeah, it's not bad. Pretty fun sometimes, and I get to leave early cause I go to work at 4:30 in the morning. So, every afternoon is like a vacation. I go to the beach after work."

He didn't tell her how he had lived in New York City before, running sound in clubs, or how he had landed a sound tech job with John Zorn, then Herbie Hancock, or about the tours he'd gone on in Europe, Australia, and Japan, with the jazz greats he'd dreamed of meeting as a teenager. That was before his body went to trash. He didn't tell her his father had called him a roadie. Or how his mother blamed everything on 'rock-n-roll.' He did not mention how he hated living in Florida, or why he stayed. His old life was over. He couldn't travel, not anymore; it was too hard.

They loaded her car, and she rattled on about the greatness of the Sunshine Hello Morning Show. To Saman's surprise, after only five minutes in the car, Thelma turned down a narrow, paved road nestled among towering, glass condos. They entered a large parking lot hidden from the main street by enormous trees.

"What is this place?" Saman asked.

"You're in for a treat if you've never been here," Thelma said, parking the car.

"I haven't. Is it a public park?" He looked around in amazement. Who knew there was a forest in downtown Fort Lauderdale?

"Nope, it's called the Bonnet House. It's an old mansion that someone converted into a museum. But it's huge. There are tons of spots where we can sneak away."

He cocked his head to the side. "Sneak away?"

"For the photo," she flirted back.

His mood lifted. She was cute, though starting to show her age, with thin crow's feet extending from each eye when she smiled, but the tropical sun did that to everyone. At least she did not look like the fake Florida girls, with puffy lips and blocky, artificial eyebrow tattoos. She looked like she spent a lot of time outside. *Make the best of things.* He reminded himself. *Make the best of right now.*

As they walked up to the entrance of the museum, Saman caught a monkey out of the corner of his eye, watching them, sitting on a tree branch.

"Look, look." He grabbed Thelma's arm and pointed to the monkey. "Are you kidding me? There are monkeys!"

"Maybe someone's escaped pet? That's the first one I've ever seen."

He took out his phone and zoomed in on the monkey, snapping a photo. "So, you've been here before?"

"Yes, a few years ago, and yesterday to scout out the location."

"Oh wow, that's so sweet of you. Here let me carry more stuff."

She handed him a bag, and they headed down a gravel walkway.

The Bonnet House resembled the farm where they had met at the San Pedro ceremony. The ambiance of old Florida pervaded both properties, cement walls painted bright yellow, ornate railings, limestone tiles, and mature trees with gray moss draped in tendrils from their bows.

A paved courtyard with pillars and hanging orchids led to the main house, a grand, cement building with windows, columns, alcoves and open rooms full of antique furniture. Beyond the house, the path turned from pavers to gravel, then to dirt.

They entered a forest of giant Banyan trees, their roots dangling in the air, twisted ropes flung over their branches. The temperature cooled under the shade of the dense canopy. Slivers of sunlight filtered through the leaves. Bugs and lizards darted around them. How could this entire forest exist unknown in Fort Lauderdale, among the tall hotels, Holiday Inns and Best Westerns, the Spring Breakers with their Jell-O shots and electric scooters? His spirit lifted. Peace permeated his body. Gratitude radiated through him.

"It's beautiful here," Saman said.

"I know. I need to come more often."

"Thank you," he said in a whisper, not caring if Thelma heard him.

They diverted off the trail, through the woods to a sparkling, blue river.

"You've got to be kidding me," Saman said.

Thelma smiled.

Water, white with the sun's reflection, peeked through the palm trees on the opposite side of the riverbank.

"Is that the ocean?" Saman asked. "I didn't realize how far east we'd come."

"No, that's the Intracoastal."

"So, this is saltwater?"

"Brackish." She nudged his arm and grinned. "Did you think I'd feed you to the gators?"

He laughed. "You know I hadn't thought about it, but now that you mention it."

"Never," she laughed, "I'm the last person you'll find in the gator swamp."

"You didn't grow up here, right?"

"No, I grew up outside Boston, in Cambridge."

"Do you still have family there?"

"Yep, my parents, alive and well and judging me every day for living in Florida with the rest of the crazies."

"I just think of Boston as insanely cold," Saman said. "They are the crazy ones."

"Totally. I'm like, talk to me in February." Thelma pulled out the feathers and the tape.

"And Simon, he's in Boston too?" Saman asked. *Why did he keep pushing this Simon thing?* It tugged on him; he couldn't stop. "You met him in Boston?"

Thelma looked up sharply. "Okay nosey, yes, but I have no idea where he is now. He could have moved."

"Sorry, I just have a feeling; maybe he's a famous millionaire now, or he has something that belongs to you and has been dying to give it back. Is that weird?" Saman asked.

"I mean we're covering you in feathers and wading into a river because you drank magic cactus tea and had a vision. I think we are beyond worrying about 'too weird.'" Thelma replied. She handed him the bag of feathers. "Now, if you don't mind sticking the feathers on, I'll set up the camera?"

He cringed, knowing what was coming next.

"You want to take your shirt off?" she asked.

He stiffened. "Actually, I think I should leave it on."

She looked at him from where she was kneeling on the ground with her camera bag and cocked her head sideways.

"In my vision, I had a black shirt on," he lied.

"Oh, I imagined you with your shirt off."

"Perv," he joked.

She giggled. "Well, I stand corrected."

He breathed a shallow sigh of relief, so she wouldn't notice. *See, that wasn't so bad.*

She cut a piece of tape, ran it up the spine of a blue feather, and stuck it on his shoulder.

"Thank god there is no breeze. I'll help you with the feathers on your back. Let's hope no one comes around to check on us. They probably don't want people getting in the water."

"I think we are the only people on the whole property."

"Sad, too. It's a beautiful day."

She passed him the tape and scissors.

"Are we polluting if we let these feathers just float away?" Saman asked.

"I thought about that, but they are dyed turkey feathers, so I guess they will biodegrade."

"Great, I don't want to mess up this place more than humans already have."

Saman went to work attaching the feathers on his left arm, around his chest, putting the smaller ones on his stomach. He mixed blue and yellow together, rather than doing solid blocks of color.

Thelma attached her camera to a large tripod next to her

light with what he guessed was a battery pack. She moved the tripods down to the edge of the water, on the shore.

Once the light was up, Saman cut her off tiny pieces of tape, and she took them from his fingertips and placed them on his back with the care of a surgeon. There was something familiar about her, like she was a childhood friend, or the girl next door. *What a cliché*, he thought, *the girl next door*. His family had moved around so much when he was little, he couldn't remember ever living next to a girl his age.

As the sun lowered, and the light slanted sideways, Thelma slipped off her shorts to reveal a yellow bathing suit bottom. Her legs were pale, smooth and long. She removed her flip-flops and put on a pair of sandals with Velcro. Saman took off his shoes, deciding to brave the water barefoot. She led Saman, covered in feathers, in his jeans, down into the river. *I should have brought a change of clothes*, he thought, *or at least dry pants*. Preoccupied with anxiety about taking off his shirt, he had forgotten more practical matters.

She removed the camera from the tripod and carried it, careful to hold the strap up around her neck so it wouldn't get wet. He wished he had a mirror to see if he looked ridiculous or 'spectacular,' as she had said. The cold water lapped at his legs and the feathers tickled the bottom of his chin. As the river reached the waistband of his jeans, Thelma stopped him.

"Right there, that's good." She snapped a photo, looked at it, and adjusted the camera. She took more photos and checked them again.

"Hold on," she said. "Let's take your hair down."

He pulled out his ponytail and let his long hair fall around the feathers. She walked up in the water, her tank-top now wet. Her bathing suit top was yellow, with black-and-white eyeball designs. *Strange*, he thought, *but cool*.

She approached him, and he tensed as she raised her hand and tucked a piece of hair behind his ear. The proximity of her body energized him.

"Am I ready for my close-up?" He grinned.

"You sure are. Now turn a little." Snap, snap, snap. She took his shot in different positions.

"Okay," she said, "Let's start pulling them off. Actually, wait; let me get some shots of the feathers too."

"Wow, I feel like a supermodel," Saman said. Every time Thelma clicked the camera, the light on the riverbank flashed.

"I'm just glad the weather is cooperating—now we could use a breeze to blow your hair around."

She pulled a few feathers off of him and stepped back for another picture. As she moved, she lost her balance. Saman reached out to steady her. She grabbed his arm and pain shot up his bicep. He shrieked and jerked away. She stumbled forward and yelped, raising her hand in the air, to avoid getting her camera wet.

"Sorry." He grabbed her again and steadied her, "My arm is..."

She leaned back, confused.

Saman froze. *Don't ruin today.* "I have ..." he trailed off. He shut his eyes, willing the pain radiating up his body to go away.

She stared at him. "Are you okay?"

There was no delaying this any longer. The fantasy was over.

"Here, give me your hand," he said.

Puzzled, she let him guide her to his forearm. He placed her palm where she had grabbed him.

She lurched her hand back. "What is that? It feels like a

river in your arm, or more like a white water rapid." Her eyes widened.

He nodded. "It's my blood."

"Your blood? That's your blood?"

He drew her in closer, putting her hand on his arm again. This time she did not move away.

"This is insane. Can I see it? Is it like an IV?"

"Sort of—it hooks me up to dialysis." He didn't make any move to pull up his sleeve. He did not want to show her.

"Dialysis, like you have diabetes?"

The water swayed between them, sloshing the feathers around.

"I wish," he said. "I'm afraid it's a bit worse."

"What is it?"

The feathers floated down the river. Déjà vu washed over him. It was as if he had held her before, told her everything before, drifted in the river with her and the feathers, all before. *Did I see this in my vision? Was she there?*

He pulled her in closer and hugged her. It felt right. She embraced him back. The remaining feathers pressed together and fell off between them.

"I'm sorry," he whispered into her hair.

She didn't respond, but let him hold her.

"My kidneys are failing," he said. "I've got what they call end-stage renal disease."

She pulled away to look at him. "That doesn't sound good."

"No, it's not."

She dropped her arms and looked at him. "Saman, I'm so sorry. And I apologize. I'm so clumsy. God, this is the second time I've fallen all over you. I don't know what's wrong with me."

"No, it's okay. It's not your fault."

"What caused the kidney failure?"

"Bad luck, messed up genes."

"That's crazy. You look totally normal. I would have never guessed."

"I don't go around telling people."

"Is that why you went to the San Pedro ceremony?"

"Yes." He met her eyes. "I'm on a transplant list, but it's hard, you know, to wait. I was struggling to accept the situation. I hoped the ceremony would help me." He stopped. He didn't want to say what he was thinking; *to help me accept death*.

"I don't know what to say." Thelma studied his face.

"I guess that's why I was pressuring you to contact Simon," he said. "Because life is short." He gazed into her eyes. Before he could decide against it, he kissed her.

She melted into his arms and kissed him back with an intensity that sent waves of heat down his legs. They kissed, open mouths and moving tongues. She reached for the back of his head and drew him in deeper like she hadn't been kissed in weeks, maybe months, years. He wrapped his good arm around her waist, pressing his body into her stomach. They kissed again and again. She returned the pressure of his embrace, her breast against his chest.

Finally, she pulled away. "Wow, I was not expecting that."

All the feathers floated in the water. Thelma's arms lay on his forearms, a circle, trying to capture the feathers before they drifted away, but the current carried them downstream.

As he watched the feathers go, he saw himself not as the radiant bird in his vision, but as he was now, featherless, sodden, diseased, stripped of his life. The metaphor sent sadness flooding into his chest. Tears threatened to crack his composure. A black hole formed and sucked the joy out of the moment, a dark, uncontrollable bloom. Muscles tense, he backed away from the photographer girl. She gathered the last of the feathers in her top like a basket of berries. He turned and sloshed to the riverbank in his sopping wet jeans.

lone in the water, Thelma watched Saman wrap her beach towel around his hips and shimmy out of his wet jeans, careful not to expose his body or underwear. Her breath came in bursts, and her heart galloped. *Fuck, I've activated my kundalini energy.* Holding the damp feathers with one hand, she stood still. Her other arm ached with the weight of her heavy camera and lens. Saman fumbled with his pants. Thelma could not form a complete thought, much less utter a sentence.

He pulled off his t-shirt and faced Thelma. "I think I better get going."

Her eyes fixed on his arm. There was not a tube, as she had imagined—it was his vein, but larger than any normal human vein. A twisted root, it wound up his arm, not unlike those hanging from the Banyan trees encasing the river. Around the bone, it mutated and bruised his skin. Still, despite the alien bulge, he was handsome. His chest muscles formed a heart shape around his small, brown nipples. A thin streak of black, curly hair ran up the center of his abdomen, hung like the rungs of a ladder to his navel. On one end of the gnarl in his arm, a white bandage and a layer of plastic sheet and tape blocked what she imaged was an entry point.

"I can take an Uber back to my car if you want to stay longer," he said.

A cloud passed over the sun. The dream came back to Thelma. Birds flew over Saman's head. They squawked in a dark circle, moving as the body of a constricting serpent, each fowl a snake scale. She shuddered. At once she saw the totality of the creatures as a unit, and the details in each face, black and cracking beaks, their eyes like glass, like taxidermied animals, no souls.

She gasped and blinked. The vision vanished.

"Sorry, I'm sorry," she muttered. "No, don't take an Uber."

She waded to the shore of the river, climbed out and put her camera in the bag, shaking, cold and wet.

Why did he want to go now? Why were boys always so eager to leave?

"We got some beautiful pictures," she said, trying to act like everything was normal.

He shifted his weight between his legs. "Sorry, I'm just tired, maybe from the sun, or the ceremony."

"Does it hurt?" she asked and took a step toward him.

"Not really. You get used to it."

She tried not to stare at his arm. She wanted to touch him again, to feel the rushing blood under his skin. *Does all our blood flow that fast?* She wished they could go to her house and take off all their clothes. She desired to look at every inch of him, but she let him be. They packed up the light and tripod together in silence.

As they left, the gatekeeper watched them with suspicion, realizing the couple had swum in the water, Saman with only a towel around his waist.

"Thanks so much," she said as they passed, shooting the gatekeeper a smile.

Saman loaded everything into the back of her car.

She did not ask more questions about his medical condition. His complicated situation stretched beyond her capacity to understand in that moment. She drove home.

As she pulled into the parking deck, Saman turned to her.

"Listen," he said.

She put the car in park, but kept staring straight ahead. If she saw how handsome he was again, she would want him even more.

"You really don't have to explain," she said. "This was just a crazy day and something happened. It's not a big deal. I need a boyfriend like I need a hole in my head."

He looked at his hands folded in his lap. "I shouldn't have kissed you. It's not fair to anyone for me to get involved with them right now."

She nodded. "I'll send you the best of the pictures. I can text you a link." She wanted to cry. It felt like they were breaking up before they even began dating.

"That would be great," Saman said.

She made herself look at him and saw his face—pinched and pained, the way she felt. She touched his good arm.

"We can just be friends. It doesn't have to go beyond that."

"Sure." He gazed out the windshield of the front of the car.

She scrambled to find words to fill the strange gap growing between them, like the better they knew each other, the farther they moved apart. It was as if he had a glass case around him. She craved to punch it and crack it, to pull him out of it, to bring him closer to her.

"And listen," she said, breathless, "the thing with Simon, I wasn't completely honest with you. It's just that, that—" She took a deep breath. *Why am I telling him this?* she wondered, but she couldn't stop. "Simon was more than a mentor. We had an affair, but he was so much older than me, and married, and I was really young. His wife found out, and they had a kid already, so I didn't want to be that girl, you know?" She pushed a stray hair out of her face. "Sorry, is that like too much drama to explain all at once?"

Saman nodded. "I figured there was more to the story."

She looked at his arm. "There always is. Right?" She wanted to tell him about the birds and the hospital and the vision that wouldn't go away, but it all was too much of a story.

"I guess so," he said. The humid air hung thick between them like steam off boiling water.

Should she try to kiss him again? Would that turn the day around?

Thelma touched his leg. "So, can we be friends?"

He paused. "Sure."

Then he got out of the car and left.

Thelma sat in the hot car alone, deflated. *At least he could have helped me carry the lights upstairs,* she thought. Tears came hot and fast to her eyes, dampening her sun-kissed cheeks. Her stomach rumbled. Multiple emotions pulled at her. She was used to feeling nothing, but now she felt everything. Why had she said the boyfriend thing? Saman wasn't trying to be her boyfriend. *Stupid, so stupid,* she thought. *Why are my instincts always wrong?*

She rubbed her hands over her face, wiping away the tears. Her damp bathing suit and the wet car seat were the only things keeping the temperature bearable. She pulled out her cell phone and stared at it. She wanted to call Saman and ask him to come back to her house, but she would look desperate.

She sighed and opened Facebook. Finding Simon's profile, she called him on messenger.

Pick up the phone.

"Hello Bella," his deep, smooth voice would say, but the phone kept ringing. Nothing but ringing.

She was about to click to end the call, when a young woman said, "Hello, can I help you?"

The phone crackled. "Hello?" the voice again.

Thelma caught her breath. "Is this Simon Amalfitano's phone?"

Static again.

"Hello?" the young woman said. "Hello?"

Hang up now, Thelma thought, but instead she threw the car door open and bolted out of the parking deck to get better reception.

On a patch of grass outside, she clutched her cell phone like a life raft. "I'm trying to reach Simon Amalfitano."

"And who am I speaking with?"

Was this Simon's wife? But the voice sounded too young.

"This is Amy." She scrambled for a name. "I'm a former student of Simon's."

Silence on the other line.

"Are you Simon's wife?" Thelma asked.

"No, I'm his daughter," the young woman said.

Thelma's mind reeled, trying to calculate the age of the woman on the phone. During their affair, Simon's daughter must have been eight or nine, maybe even ten, which would mean now she was twenty or so. The idea brought Thelma to the ground. She sat in her bikini bottom and top on the grass. His daughter had grown up and become a woman, but what had Thelma accomplished in the same amount of time? Not the gallery shows she had dreamed of, or the meaningful art Simon had believed her capable of creating.

"Is your father around?" Thelma managed. "Or could I get his phone number? I'd love to catch up with him."

The girl did not respond.

Thelma kept talking, "Or I could leave you my number and he could call me back?"

Silence on the other line. Had her bad mobile service disconnected them? "Hello?" she said. "Are you still there?"

"Yes, sorry. I'm sorry, I'm still processing all of this myself."

Processing all of this? The phrase sounded wrong. *Processing what?* The phone call? Where was Simon? The dread from her vision crept into her chest, the hospital bed, but no, it could not be true.

"I'm very sorry to tell you," the girl said, "but, I guess you haven't heard the news, but Simon was in an accident. He is . . . he is in a coma."

"A coma?"

His daughter sighed. "He's in a vegetative state."

"Oh, my god." Thelma reeled. This was not happening. *This could not be happening.*

"I'm afraid so."

"I'm so sorry." Tears rolled down Thelma's cheeks. "I just can't believe this."

"I can't either."

Thelma wiped her eyes. "When did it happen?"

"November 10th, just two weeks ago. He was biking to campus, to teach his night class. A car hit him." Simon's daughter choked on the words. "It knocked him into the middle of the intersection." Her voice broke with emotion.

Thelma gasped. *A bike?* She never knew Simon to ride a bike. Time had passed, she supposed. She pictured Simon on a bike, in the cold, New York autumn, on campus, in a sweater—no, a long coat. She crumpled forward, hugging her knees. How could this be happening?

"I'm so, so sorry," Thelma said.

"I'm sorry. I'm actually at the hospital now with him," his daughter said, pulling herself together. "I should let you go, but if he wakes up, I'll tell him you called. What is your name again?" The fatigue and grief in her voice told the story of a woman facing a long night.

"Amy Chenoweth." Thelma used her real last name. Simon would know it was her. "And, sorry but which hospital?" Thelma asked. "I'll send some flowers. I would like to do that. That is the least I could do."

"Thank you. He's in Mount Sinai, Room 4119, in New York City."

"And sorry, remind me what your name is?" Try as she might, Thelma she could not remember the daughter's name.

"It's Raquel."

"Thank you, Raquel. Again, I'm so, so sorry."

She hung up. Stunned, Thelma pushed herself off the ground and went back to her car to get her camera bags.

November 10th, November 10th, why did that date sound so familiar?

Then she realized; it was the date of the San Pedro ceremony.

Her world slipped out of focus, broken blue and green bokeh. *Simon. Simon. Simon.* She wanted to scream his name, for him to hear her through the fog of wherever he was, lost in a coma. A coma? How could this be happening? The

beige paint of the parking deck walls moved to her periph-
ery. Her mind emptied.

I'm cracking up.

She slugged across the cement lot, dazed and robotic,
one foot in front of the other, until she reached her
bedroom. The empty plastic feather bags, still on her duvet
from the photoshoot, crumpled and crackled under her
weight as she threw her body onto the bed. She rolled up in
the covers and clenched her pillow between her fists. Her
sobs tore the room's silence, like rips in the atmosphere.

6

S aman wondered if one day StanGetz would eat his dead body. He stroked the gray cat's cheek in a wiping motion. Would he collapse in his living room, or at the kitchen table? Would his mother find him and Stan, hungry, having a last supper together, only not together, one of them gone? He tried not to fixate on these dark ideas, but they came to him nonetheless. StanGetz snuggled closer to Saman. He used to never cuddle, but sensing a change in his caretaker, the cat came in the evenings and sat on his lap, watching TV with him in bed, before he went to sleep.

Saman wished sometimes that he could pour himself a bourbon, or maybe five bourbons, one after another, in a whiskey glass, cover the ice with the brown liquid and drink them down until he faded away and forgot the world. He tried a few times to numb himself, once with vodka, once with gin, rationalizing that it would be easier and faster to use hard liquor, but each time it only increased the pain in his abdomen and heightened his anxiety. It wasn't worth it. So, he tried Prozac, Lexapro, Zoloft, and anti-anxiety medications whose names he could not remember. His depression waned on the pills, but his constant worry about sudden death increased.

He pet StanGetz and stared at his TV's blank screen. The cat purred and squeezed his eyes shut. He'd moved the TV from the living room to the bedroom, to be more comfortable, but it hurt his neck to watch the large TV lying down. The TV cost double what he'd planned to spend on it, convinced by the sales guy to buy the higher-resolution model, so he'd better watch it, Goddammit.

Some days he sat in bed with StanGetz until he was ready to sleep. He clicked through the TV channels. He swiped left and right on his phone, looking at pictures of the beautiful, young women, Venezuelan, Cuban, and Brazilian girls, that he would never message, much less date. He'd given up on reading books. When he did not have to go to the hospital for dialysis, he preferred to stay with StanGetz, in the safety of his room, where he could contort his body into whatever position he wanted, and wear whatever he wanted, trying to find peace from the gnawing pain that plagued him, and from his thoughts, which were worse to cope with than the physical pain.

He glanced at his phone. No calls. No new messages.

I mean why would she call? After how you left? Why would anyone call? I'm probably just clinically depressed right now, he thought, *but these problems are in perpetuity.*

He sighed.

Regret, he thought, *that is another topic altogether.*

The bedroom needed dusting. He considered hiring a cleaning lady because he was too tired to clean himself, but every cent he made paid for his treatments at the hospital. The radio station insurance had high deductibles and high copays. He ran up credit cards, with the plan to never pay them off, figuring he would die before the collectors could get him.

His mom came over sometimes to help clean and cook.

"Saman," she would say, "look at this filth. Are you doing drugs? Why don't you get the home treatment? What have you eaten today? Have you gone to the dentist? Any news from the donor list? Your father would hate to see you like this."

Her questions bothered him more than the dust on the dresser did.

Who gives a fuck about the dentist when you're one missed dialysis treatment away from a funeral?

Saman packed marijuana into a navy-blue bong he kept by his bed. Green-and-black resin coated the inside of the glass, one more item he wouldn't be cleaning. Smoking pot was not necessarily the best thing he could do for his condition, but he rationalized it wasn't the worst either. It was better than drinking and committing suicide; those were other options.

StanGetz stood up and stretched his back, giving a quiet meow to Saman as he moved out of his comfortable sleeping spot to accommodate the bong.

"Time to get high, Stan," Saman said and lit the weed.

He loved the ritual of smoking—the sound of the lighter, his breath drawing in, the bubbles in the bong's basin of water, the smoke filling up the neck before he inhaled in a gush of heat and cleared the chamber.

He held in the marijuana until his lungs burned, then exhaled the white smoke. Leaning back in bed, he repeated the process—click, bubble, whoosh, ah. He was high. Returning the bong to his bedside table, Saman sank deeper into the cocoon of his comforter. He liked to turn up the air conditioner. The cold air helped him feel better. Whenever he got too hot, his skin began to itch, another side-effect of his nonfunctioning kidneys. They called the itching syndrome *pruritus*. *What a nice-sounding name for a shitty condition*, he thought, moving lower on his pillow. StanGetz curled in a neat ball of gray fur next to his hip.

Some days the weed evicted his anxiety and other days it made it worse, but at least it was a change. It helped with wanting to eat. Saman caressed his cat's back and thought about what to make for dinner. Meal planning was an enemy. Everything he put in his body had to be tracked and monitored to comply with his renal failure diet. He needed to eat fresh meat, eight to ten ounces a day, and consume exactly four cups of liquid a day. Gone were his morning coffees out of a barrel-sized metal thermos. Gone was drinking Bud Light all afternoon by the pool with his friends, or margaritas at the beach, or any of the other things he used to do on the weekends. Eating an orange was impossible. French fries, which he missed the most, were a forbidden food, along with pumpkin seeds, hot dogs, and avocados.

He cared little about social events and avoided restaurants. Following the diet was a full-time job required to keep on living. Sometimes he microwaved a baked potato and called it lunch. Dinner might be a frozen hamburger patty or a couple of chicken breasts. He hated eggs because of eating so many of them, trying to maintain his optimal protein levels

Maybe I still have a steak in the freezer, he thought. He could throw it on the stove and cook it fast.

Saman turned on the TV and flicked to the channel called 'Heroes and Icons.' StanGetz lifted his head for a second with the sound, then went back to his eyes-closed position. Heroes and Icons showed only reruns of action shows, like *Renegade* and *Rawhide*, featuring tough guys and rough women, who smoked cigarettes and drove motorcycles.

A show called *Hunter* was on, about wayward homicide detectives in Southern California. Despite the synthesizer soundtracks, or maybe because of them, Saman liked these old shows. His father, whose English was poor, watched American action movies because there was no need to understand the words. As a child, Saman would hover in the living room, behind his dad's chair, trying to catch glimpses of *MacGyver* or *Maverick* before his father would turn and yell at him in Farsi to go to the kitchen and finish his homework.

On *Hunter* now, a woman with long, red hair and pouting magenta lips stood by the edge of a swimming pool, wearing a black bikini. She shimmied her hips and said, "Come on, let's swim," trying to entice her boyfriend to jump into the water.

As the woman dove into the pool, another man emerged from the bushes holding a pistol. He shot the boyfriend. The woman rose from underwater to find her dead boyfriend, floating face-down in a halo of blood. She shrieked.

Cut to commercial.

Saman picked up his phone. There was a missed text from his older sister, Yalda. Did he want to come to his niece's ballet recital in two weeks?

Not really, he thought.

A few texts below Yalda's was his thread of messages before the photoshoot with Thelma. "Girl from San Pedro," said the contact. He opened the chain.

Why didn't I tell her what was going on, instead of acting weird?

The last woman he'd gone on a date with, months before getting the fistula in his arm, was a cute Colombian girl, a waitress at one of the dockside restaurants in Fort Lauderdale. He'd taken her for cocktails, him careful to only have one, while she had three. They'd gone dancing, at a nightclub, but the date exhausted Saman. By midnight he longed to go home. Like Thelma, he had kissed the Colombian girl goodbye, then ghosted her. She was nice and cute, but he was tired, in a terminal sense.

Flicking the phone to Facebook, he searched for Thelma. She came up, posing by a colorful graffiti wall, holding her camera and smiling. She was not his usual type. He gravitated to young, Latin women, who worked as bartenders or went to community college, who loved to dance and smile, and only cared if he paid for dinner, and bought drinks. They didn't ask too many questions.

Since he'd gotten sick, girls still tried to talk to him, girls from the radio station, from the hospital, but they turned Saman off. The women who approached him, aware of his illness, looked at him like a child's stuffed animal, something to make them feel better about their own lives. He attracted the single mothers, the ex-drug addicts, the girl's whose stepdads had molested them as children.

Then there were the women who pictured him as their latest renovation project. These 'bossgirls,' as he called them, were single, had loud voices, master's degrees, and owned houses. They thought he was their next charity gala date, a new thing to show their true compassion for the needy. Those women were the worst; they buzzed around him like bees, trying to suck nectar out of an un-blooming flower. They researched kidney donor programs and proposed crowdfunding expensive treatments or writing letters to Oprah. His older sister Yalda fell into this category too, of women who knew nothing but suggested everything.

"I've told you a million times," she would say, "you must go to Iran, and offer them US dollars. Many people there will sell you a kidney, for sure. Why haven't you gone?" Or her latest fascination with the deep web. "You can buy organs online, living ones, from the darknet," she told him.

As if he had tens of thousands of dollars to shop for illegal organs or the ability to travel. Every forty-eight hours he needed to be back at the hospital and hooked up to the dialysis machine.

He looked through Thelma's pictures, but there wasn't much to see, mostly shots of other people and portraits she had taken of couples and babies. One photo with her arm around an older man, maybe her father, another of her on skis, snow-covered peaks in the background.

Why did I even agree to take pictures with her? Still, part of him wanted to call her again. *Was it loneliness? No, it was something else. Was it the way she'd looked at him?*

He pictured her at the San Pedro ceremony where he first saw her. He had watched her all night. She sat diagonal from him in the circle, elegant and upright, tall, with her back straight and her legs crossed, her blond hair falling on her shoulders. Maybe it was just the medicine, but on the San Pedro cactus she was a luminous, peaceful being. He remembered thinking, she must meditate. While the other people around her threw up and cried, she beamed serenity.

Why did I risk contamination from the river water? Why did I agree to the photos? What did any of these visions mean?

He took another bong hit.

Maybe it was not about the way she'd looked at him; but the way he'd looked at her?

He muted *Hunter* and called her.

The phone rang three times. *Pick up, pick up,* he thought. Then, as if she heard him, she answered.

"Hello."

"Hey."

"Hi," Thelma said.

"Hey, listen, I'm so sorry about the way I left the other day."

She said nothing.

"I find it hard to talk about, but I'm really sick. I'm probably going to die sooner rather than later. I spend a lot of time at the hospital. I have to constantly take my own blood pressure. I hardly can pee. I get tired easily, and I push people away." He paused and sucked in air. "And I'm not supposed to swim, especially in non-chlorinated water, but I agreed to take those pictures because I wanted an excuse to hang out with you." He stopped, astounded by his own forthcoming. Silence filled up the bedroom like the smoke in his bong.

"Are you still there?" Saman asked. He heard something else in the background. Was it wind?

"I'm sorry," Thelma said, "I'm at a photoshoot right now at the beach."

Saman felt so dumb; he should have asked her if it was a good time to talk. "Sorry," he said. "I just wanted to let you know what was going on. I'm just being a weirdo."

"It's okay. But I should go. I can't really talk now."

"Listen, I'd really like to see you and apologize in person. Where is the shoot? I could come by after you're done."

She hesitated. "To the beach?"

"Yeah, why not?"

"It's going to be pretty late. They want to do night shots. I've got to wait on the sunset."

"I don't mind. I don't have work in the morning."

"Um, sure, Hollywood beach, at the north end, near the park."

"I'll be there. Text me thirty minutes before you're done."

They said goodbye and hung up.

His cat meowed by the door, wanting out.

"Jeez Stan," he said, "did I need to be so dramatic?"

But when you're dying at thirty-five everything is dramatic, he thought, *death is dramatic.* There was no time to waste. He got up and started to clean his bedroom.

7

Gusts of wind blew the pregnant woman's hair around her face like seaweed in waves. The client wore a red chiffon dress that kept flying up, to reveal her bathing suit bottom. Thelma wished she had rescheduled the shoot for a clearer day. Above the beach, rain threatened to pour from dark clouds.

"Turn please a little, and put out your chin," she told the young woman. "Now put your hands on your stomach."

The girl nodded. Her husband resembled an Asian Abercrombie and Fitch model. He stripped down to a pair of red bathing trunks and started doing pushups on the sand while he waited to join the picture. His wife's thirty-four-week pregnant stomach jutted out of her red dress like a half-eaten candied apple on a stick.

Thelma exchanged glances with her assistant Carlos. This would be a painful shoot.

With the wind, Thelma needed to take many shots of each pose to get even one that looked natural. She'd wanted to put bobby pins in the woman's hair to keep it out of her face, but the lady had refused. There would be a lot of bad images to sift through in the edit. Then again, at least the hefty breeze and the whitecaps on the waves cleared the shoreline of tourists. Thelma could focus without pausing for children to run by with buckets, or girls in thong bikinis taking selfies in the background.

The sunlight shifted between angry clouds, creating another problem for Thelma: changing light conditions. Carlos moved a portable light, trying to help, but it was a time-consuming endeavor. She feared the battery pack powering the light would run out of juice before she could finish.

"Right there please," she shouted to Carlos over the wind. Carlos was a great assistant, still in high school, but he wanted to be a photographer himself. Thelma was grateful his parents let him work for her part-time.

Ever since talking to Raquel, all she could think about was Simon. Researching the hit-and-run online, she had found nothing. She struggled to concentrate on the photographs. Should she tell Saman about the vision of the birds and Simon's coma?

The woman leaned against the man's chest, and Thelma moved around them with her camera, running through a mental list as she worked—close-ups, mid-shot, wide-shot, hands-on-stomach, singles of her alone, them kissing, her looking back at him, him looking at her. *What else was there?*

She checked the sun. It was setting behind the trees that lined the beach. Soon it would be dark. She would take a few more shots, then send this couple on their way. She liked this part of the coast, because the nature preserve hid all the cheap hotels and the towering condominiums full of Quebecois snowbirds.

She turned to her assistant, "Okay, let's set up for the night shots."

Carlos lowered the light stand.

"You guys can take a quick break," she told the couple. They adjusted their outfits and looked at their phones.

"Can we do some in the water?" the pregnant woman asked.

"Sure, but then your clothes will be wet for the rest of the shots, so maybe do it last?"

"No, I'm going in my bathing suit." The girl stripped out of her dress, revealing a red thong bikini. Glitter surrounded her extended belly button.

Of course you are, Thelma thought. *Baywatch here we come.* She exchanged another knowing glance with Carlos who grinned.

"Don't go too far out, please," Thelma said. "There is a mean undertow."

Dusk dropped and Thelma took the rest of the shots. Midway through her night sequences, she turned around to get a different lens out of her bag and there was Saman, standing by the boardwalk, a shadow-figure, watching her work.

Thelma's body tingled. Her face flushed. He waved at her and she wanted to crumble into the sand like a kicked-over castle.

Why does he have to be so goddamn handsome?

Her palms sweating, she finished the photos.

"Thanks guys. I'll be back to you with the shots early next week."

Saman stood by her camera bag, smiling.

"Hey," Thelma said.

The bikini couple gathered their things.

"Hey yourself." Saman stepped forward and hugged her. She wondered if he could feel her heart pounding through her shirt.

"Thelma, do you want me to pack these lights in the car?" Carlos asked from behind her. He squinted at Saman, trying to get a good look at him in the dark.

"No thanks, that's okay."

Carlos shrugged, then gave her a miniature salute and headed off.

Thelma turned to Saman. Before she could put down her camera, or think or speak or even breath, his lips were on hers, kissing her, hot, eager and hungry. She sank with him into the sand. They made out in the dark like two teenagers at summer camp. He smelled of grass and incense and the sea.

What am I doing? she thought.

Lying by the ocean, they kissed until her mouth hurt. Finally pulling away, Thelma gazed into Saman's eyes.

"It's getting cold." Saman rubbed Thelma's shoulder. She snuggled closer to him.

"We're covered in sand," she said.

He hugged her to his chest. "Should we go back to my house?" he asked. "It's not that far from here."

She hesitated. She had so many questions about his kidney condition, but it would destroy the moment. He would get up, or he would leave again, and she never wanted him to leave.

"I don't know," she said. "I've been going nuts since the ceremony."

"What do you mean?" He looked concerned. "Like the San Pedro made you feel bad?"

"No, not like nuts like I'm depressed or bipolar or something, I mean I feel happy and I've had more energy than ever."

"So, what's going on?" He put his hand on her stomach.

She took a deep breath. "I had another vision, in a dream, and I got in touch with Simon."

Saman sat up. "Really? What happened?"

"It's really crazy."

"Tell me everything," he said, pulling his hair back into a ponytail.

She described her vision of Simon in the hospital and seeing Saman below the window, the blackbirds and her fear in the dream. He furrowed his brow and let her finish, without interrupting her. She couldn't tell if he looked troubled or patient, it was too dark.

"But that's not all. So, I called Simon's phone again, and his daughter answered and she said he's—" she stopped. Thelma held back tears. Every time she thought of Simon, lying in the intersection of the wet street, headlights running around him, his life knocked out, she wanted to cry.

"You can tell me," Saman said. He squeezed her hand.

"His daughter told me . . ." Thelma took a deep breath. "His daughter said there was an accident and Simon's in a coma. Like what I saw, that was real." The words caught in her throat. She had been thinking them, but to say them out loud was something else entirely.

"Holy fuck."

"This has never happened to me before, not like I've been experiencing this kind of stuff on a regular basis."

"The San Pedro," Saman said. "That is some crazy shit."

"Not only that, but the accident was on the same day as the San Pedro ceremony. It is really crazy."

"And the black birds," Saman said. "It's like you knew I was sick."

Thelma nodded. "The birds were really scary. I was trying to yell at you to warn you, but you weren't listening."

She closed her eyes. When she opened them, Saman was up and dusting sand off himself.

"We should call Maria and try to talk to the shaman."

"It opened up some temporary channel or something." Thelma stood up too and brushed herself off.

"You saw the vision before we went to the Bonnet House, right?" he asked.

"I was going to tell you, but you left."

"I know. I wish I hadn't." He reached for her hand.

He still had his bracelet on from the ceremony, and so did she.

"Let's go back to my place," he said. "I'll call Maria, see if we can talk to the shaman."

Thelma had not thought to call the shaman. What would he say? Did he hear about this stuff all the time? She picked up her camera bag. "Okay. I've just been freaking out, but you're right, I should talk to someone."

"And I'm glad you told me." He kissed her again. Thelma relaxed for the first time in days. They hugged, and he held her tight against him.

"Thank you," he whispered into her ear.

"For what?" she whispered back.

"For waking me up from my own bad dream." He stepped back from the hug and looked at her.

"That's not dramatic at all." Thelma raised her eyebrows.

"Well look, now we've got comas, kidneys, shamans and scary birds. Past dramatic don't you think?" He cocked his head and winked. "All we need now is an alien spaceship to appear."

Thelma laughed. The two made their way back to the parking lot under the tilted eye of the crescent moon.

SAMAN AND THELMA drove west from Fort Lauderdale towards the Everglades. The farther they got away from the city, the more Thelma's anxiety increased. She could not shake the image of the birds over Saman's head.

Am I conjuring this myself? she wondered.

Or if she channeled the vision, like a radio receiver, picking up the airwaves of spirits, then why now, and why this? How could she have known about Simon? This was the question that haunted her. *Was it all a coincidence? Was this all part of the wachuma ceremony?*

"I never believed I was special or clairvoyant or anything," she told Saman. "We used to have sleepovers and the girls would do Ouija Boards and I always thought it was stupid."

"What's a Ouija Board?" Saman asked.

"It's a board game that is supposed to be an oracle."

"My mother thinks you can tell your fortune from the patterns in your coffee cup." Saman shook his head.

"What?"

"Yeah, it's a Persian thing, reading your coffee."

"How does that work? Like you make a latte and read your foam?"

"No, like women get together and they drink Turkish coffee in these little cups." he made an inch shape with his fingers. "Then when you finish your coffee, you leave some in the cup. They put a saucer over it and turn it upside down. Then they look at the pattern the coffee leaves behind."

"Fortune tellers do this?"

Saman chuckled. "No, whichever woman thinks she's the best at reading the cups will look at everyone's and then they will see the pattern and be like, 'Oh look, I see a ring,'" He put on a thick Iranian accent and spoke in falsetto like a woman, teasing Thelma. "That means a good man is coming into your life." He poked her in the side.

"We should do that!" Thelma laughed. "That sounds so fun."

"It's just a way to give people compliments. They never say anything bad. It's always like you're going to find love, or get money, or have a baby."

"No crazier than palm reading, I guess," Thelma said. She pulled the car off the highway and they sat on the exit ramp, waiting for the light to turn green.

"One of my mother's friends once told me I would live a long healthy life and be a doctor," Saman added. "Guess my kidneys weren't communicating through the coffee very well that day." He looked out the window of the car.

Thelma scowled. "Or she's right, and you will." She glanced over at Saman. "I mean, not the doctor part."

Why does he have to be so morbid, Thelma wondered, *always thinking about death?* She searched her brain—had she known anyone else with a serious medical condition? She tried to think. None of her friends growing up had died or were sick, and her relatives were all healthy. Two of her grandparents had died before she was born, but her remaining grandparents were both in good shape for their ages. Her grandmother lived in Boston near her parents, and still spent every summer sailing and lounging on the beach in Martha's Vineyard, drinking wine with her friends. Her grandfather stayed with his new wife in Virginia. He had needed hip surgery a few years back, but that was all, and now, though he walked with a cane, he never talked about death or his old age. He followed politics and loved to watch C-SPAN. She wished she could see them both more often and made a mental note to call them next week.

As they headed off the highway, the landscape evolved

from gray to green. Thelma, following the GPS directions
for the address given to them by Maria, turned down a
narrow road, lined on both sides by mailboxes and wood
fences. Fruit trees and overgrown grass grew around older
ranch-style houses, mixed in between massive, white and
pink villas with columns and vines crawling along their
edges.

They parked at a sprawling villa, hidden behind a
circular driveway and a high, stone gate. On the edge of
the Everglades, the old house was in various stages of
construction. Scaffolding held up cement pillars. Stray
cats roamed the yard and posed like statues on the front
steps. Thick vegetation, trees, and hanging vines
surrounded the house. It reminded Thelma of *The Jungle
Book*, or *Indiana Jones*, if she could replace the cats with
monkeys.

Maria, the shaman's translator from the ceremony, came
out of the front door and greeted the couple in the driveway.

"Welcome, please my loves, please come inside," Maria
said, her voice lilted with a heavy Spanish accent. She wore
a long white skirt and a blue blouse with flowers embroidered on the collar. She was a short, older woman, but trim,
and youthful in her step.

Maria opened the door and led them inside. Taita Diego,
the shaman from the ceremony, greeted them with open
arms and a cacophony of barking, tiny Pomeranian puppies
at his feet.

"Bienvenidos a todos!" he bellowed.

Saman burst out laughing.

The puppies barked and jumped like spit on a skillet,
nipping at Thelma's ankles.

"Oh my god," she said. There must have been ten or
twelve puppies. She could not believe what she was seeing.

"Are these your puppies?" She laughed and tried to grab one, but it bounced away like a rubber ball.

"No, no," Maria said to the puppies. "Down, down."

The shaman belly-laughed and said something in Spanish. Saman bent down to pet the puppies. They swarmed onto him, each eager to climb up into his lap.

"They are so cute," Saman said.

"They belong to the owner of the house," Maria said. "A friend of the shaman's."

"Oh, the shaman doesn't live here?" Thelma asked.

"Oh no, no, Taita Diego lives in Ecuador. He's just visiting." Maria translated what she'd said to the shaman. He nodded and beamed a smile.

The puppies quieted but continued to wag their tiny tails and scamper about the feet of their visitors.

"I love Florida," Taita Diego said, making out the foreign words as best he could. "But my English not so good." He grinned and shrugged, lifting his two hands up as if to say, 'oh well.'

The foyer of the house opened to a living room with a black leather sofa, an enormous television set on a dusty stand, and a long, glass coffee table with Lucite legs. A life-size, framed painting of Jesus, his hands in prayer, hung on the wall. Unlike the modern, white Miami condos, the house was dark and musty, with hardwood floors. The scent of the puppies and their training papers mingled with the faint smell of mildew.

Taita Diego was a different person without his ceremonial robes. He wore an old Miami Dolphins baseball cap, khaki shorts, and a faded, gray University of Miami t-shirt, with a stretched neckline. Though his eyes twinkled, he could have been anyone, the guy beside you in line at Wal-

Mart, a neighbor watering their lawn. He was as ordinary as any man could be.

Is this all a scam? Thelma wondered. What made a man a shaman? She wished she had read more about shamanism and Ecuador. Again, she felt like an imposter, just an ignorant American girl, with her bad Spanish and incapacity to remember any Latin America history. Had she even learned Latin America history in school? She tried to retrieve the name of the capital city of Ecuador from her memory, or any city in Ecuador, but she could not, not one. *Cuernavaca?* No, that was in Mexico.

Interrupting her thoughts, in a sudden, exaggerated motion, Taita Diego leaped to his tiptoes, shot his arms up in the air, then hunched down like a large bear and chased after the puppies, growling and making roaring noises. The puppies went wild, shrieking and scampering in all directions. He lunged after them and rounded them up in his big arms, carrying them off to a room at the end of the hall which he blockaded with a wooden baby gate. The puppies bounced and barked behind the barrier.

Thelma's jaw drooped. Saman giggled at Taita Diego, who skipped down the hall, clowning with his visitors, a jovial grin on his face.

"Come, sweetie." Maria put her hand on Thelma's shoulder. "Let's sit outside and you tell us what is troubling you."

8

Thick, green grass framed a rectangular swimming pool in the backyard. The group sat on outdoor sofas under a cement awning. An upright piano stood by the entrance to the patio. Saman wondered if the piano was for parties, imagining poolside BBQs and children's birthdays with piñatas.

Thelma explained her visions to the shaman and Maria, the ceremony, Simon's name, meeting Saman, and the hospital room. She paused between sentences to allow Maria to translate.

Thelma's voice cracked as she described the birds over Saman's head.

Saman jumped in, "And the thing is, I have kidney failure, but Thelma did not know that when she had those visions."

"My dear boy." Maria leaned forward and touched Saman's hand. "During the ceremony, I thought about you the whole time. When I saw your number on my phone, my heart jumped. I was worried something had happened to you." She tapped her chest with her palm and shook her head. "I am so glad you were fine, and that you two found good company with each other."

Saman squeezed Thelma's hand. "Thank you," he said. "I appreciate that."

Taita Diego listened without comment.

"I should add," Saman said, "that I told Thelma about my vision, of myself in a river, covered in feathers, so maybe she saw the birds because of hearing that?"

"It still doesn't explain how I knew Simon was in a coma." She looked at the shaman. "I came to the San Pedro ceremony and asked for clarity, but all I got was confusion."

Taita Diego watched and listened to her with deep concentration.

"And now I'm more confused than ever," Thelma continued. "I don't want to use the word unstable, because I don't think I'm crazy, but the world seems unstable, like I'm missing something important, like something bad is going to happen." She sighed.

"Oh sweetie, don't worry," Maria said, wringing her hands together. "Your clairvoyance is a blessing."

Thelma nodded, but Saman could see the weight of her visions in her eyes. Describing the dreams out loud made their prophetic nature more real. She was pale and tired. He slid his arm around her shoulder. He had chosen on the beach that night to stop fearing the future. He could be selfish. He would spend time with her until things ended.

Maria moved and knelt on the ground by Thelma's knee. "Sweetie, you have a gift. You must be open to the unknown. With openness, you can integrate your experience."

Thelma did not look reassured; she remained on the edge of tears.

Taita Diego asked Maria something in Spanish.

"He wants to know what you do for work?" Maria asked Thelma.

"I'm a photographer," Thelma said.

"Ah," Taita Diego spoke, "una fótógrapha." He nodded. He stared at Thelma while he spoke more in Spanish.

Maria translated, "He says that it makes sense for you to have such vivid and detailed visions because of your photography work. The part of your brain that looks at images is more developed than other people's. Grandfather medicine teaches through your own language. A writer finds a story in words, a musician hears music, an engineer learns through geometry and buildings. You see visuals because you understand the vocabulary of pictures." Maria sat back.

"But I don't understand them," Thelma said, "and it's like the ceremony never ended. I keep seeing things."

"You asked to see your path, and the medicine showed you Simon's name," Maria translated as the shaman spoke. "Then you saw Simon again in the hospital. That is your path. You must go to see Simon."

Saman tensed up, startled by the directness of Taita Diego's words. There was something about the phrase, *You asked to see your path*. It sounded wrong to him. He did not want her to see Simon, and in a coma, what was the point?

Thelma stiffened. "In person? I don't know if that's a good idea."

"That is what the medicine has revealed," Maria said. "Who was Simon to you? Can you tell us about the last time you saw him?"

Yes, Saman thought, *let's hear this.*

"Let me think." Thelma said, "The last time?" She closed her eyes. "I had gone to Paris to study art history, and he came to visit me. We said goodbye at the airport. That was the last time I saw him."

"And you loved him very much?" Maria asked.

"Yes, I did." Emotion washed over her face and she bowed her head.

Saman scowled. If Thelma still loved Simon after all this time, then she would always love him. *She will continue, but I will die soon*, he thought. It was terribly unfair. *Shit man, how many times a day do you think about death?* He hated how pessimistic he'd become.

Maria pulled a tissue out of her purse and handed it to Thelma.

"Don't cry, my dear. This is the medicine's purpose: to find your rough spots, bring them to the surface and rub them out."

Blowing her nose, Thelma said, "But I feel like I saw him last week. It was so real. Does this ever happen to you?" She looked back and forth at Maria and Taita Diego.

Saman's arms itched, and the conversation tired him. *I need to eat something,* he thought. *Have I eaten today?* He tried to remember, but nothing came to him.

Taita Diego spoke and Maria translated, "Love lost to circumstance is a powerful condition; it can cause grief as strong as bereavement. The medicine showed your unresolved emotions about Simon." Maria gestured to Saman. "To move on, you must deal with your grief."

Saman gauged Thelma's reaction, but she looked hardened and stoic, in denial of Taita Diego's conclusion. She clung to her efforts not to cry. Maria raised her eyebrows at Saman, as if to say, *See what I mean?*

She is stuck, Saman thought.

"I haven't thought about Simon in years," Thelma said.

"You don't have to think," Maria said. She tapped her palm to her chest. "Your body knows."

Part of Saman felt betrayed. Thelma had described Simon as a mentor. Had he ever been her teacher at all? Why had she lied? What else was she hiding?

Taita Diego stood and went to the edge of the pool. He gazed at the clear, cobalt water. After a moment he spoke, with Maria translating.

"There is an old children's story," he said, "about a cactus who wanted to become a man. The cactus watched all the Indian families, and he wanted to have a wife and children, because he lived alone and not even a bird would sit on his branches."

Taita Diego looked at Saman, then at Thelma. "So, one day the cactus called to some children, 'Hey children, bring me your father's hat, I want to become a man.' And the children brought him the hat, but he still felt like a cactus, so he said, 'I need a shirt. Please children, can you bring me a shirt?' So, the children brought him their father's shirt and put it on the cactus. Still, the cactus was not satisfied. He said, 'Listen, please, bring me your baby brother, I want to hold him and feel what it is to have a family and be a man.'"

Saman leaned back. *Where is this story going?*

The shaman continued, powerful and fierce as he spoke, despite his plain clothes. "While the children's mother fetched water, the children took their baby brother from his basket and placed him on the cactus's branch. The baby boy screamed and cried and blood rushed forth from his body, pierced by the cactus's quills. And still, the cactus did not feel like a man. The children, afraid, ran and hid. Their mother came back and found the baby basket empty. She looked for her children and found them acting strange, so she whipped them until they confessed. It was too late. She ran out to find the cactus, but her baby boy had bled out and died. She took the baby from the branch of thorns and fell to the ground, holding the dead infant. She screamed and cried, cursing her own children for what they'd done. As she wailed, the cactus said, '*Hello, have you come to be my wife? I want to become a man.*' When the mother heard these words, she looked up and saw that the cactus wore her husband's clothes. Hatred flashed in her eyes like a summer thunderstorm. She went and got an ax. She chopped the cactus down to strings and fibers, so hacked apart that not even birds could build a nest from the tatters."

The sun shone on Taita Diego's back, shadowing his face. He bowed his head in prayer.

Saman wanted to leave. He was dizzy and hot. *Did I take my blood pressure this morning?* he wondered. He could not remember.

Thelma, confused, looked to Saman for what to do, but he shook his head.

What the fuck was that story supposed to mean? Saman wondered.

The four of them remained in silence until Taita Diego said, "You have heard from grandfather, now it is time to listen to grandmother."

Saman leaned forward. He knew what 'listen to grandmother' meant.

"Thelma, have you eaten pork or drank alcohol this week?" Maria asked.

Thelma shook her head no.

"What about antidepressants? Are you on any medications?"

Thelma frowned. "No, just birth control pills. Why?"

"We have a grandmother ceremony tonight on the same farm where you took the San Pedro. I think your friend

Camilla is planning on attending. It would be good for you to come."

"Grandmother medicine? Is that ayahuasca?" Thelma asked.

Maria nodded. "Yes, ayahuasca. It is a vine and a leaf. We mix them, from the Amazon. Very powerful medicine for seeing and healing."

Grandmother. Saman leaned back on the sofa. He had wanted to try the grandmother medicine, the ayahuasca, but Maria had warned him against attending a grandmother ceremony. Even with the San Pedro ceremony, Maria had cautioned him, but he had insisted. After some research, Taita Diego allowed him to join the San Pedro ceremony. Others in Ecuador had taken the San Pedro while on dialysis and had been fine. But would they agree for him to take the grandmother medicine? Ayahuasca was harder on the stomach and more intense than San Pedro.

"It is a different Taita, not me, but very good," Taita Diego said in broken English. "That is my advice." Then he spoke in Spanish to Maria.

Maria stood up. "Taita Diego would like to cleanse you with the *Agua de Florida*. He thanks you for coming and he hopes to see you again soon."

Thelma and Saman stood up, side by side, facing the pool with their arms outstretched, palms upward to receive the cleansing liquid. Taita Diego drank the Florida water from a small, glass bottle with a gold top, and then spit the fluid onto them. It smelled like men's cologne. Saman imagined that it must taste terrible.

As Taita Diego finished, Saman noticed a thin, dirt path, at the back edge of the yard behind the shaman. The trail beckoned to him, winding up into the Everglades, then dropping out of sight beyond the brush.

"Para los caballos," Taita Diego said, pointing to the trail, following Saman's gaze.

"Ca-by-yos?" Thelma said, struggling to pronounce the word.

"The horses," Saman said. "Caballos is horses in Spanish."

"Yes," Maria said, "there are wild caballos. They come to the pool; maybe we see one."

Saman marveled at the veritable jungle. The tiny path filled him with the awe of a child finding a secret treehouse. He remembered how his father had told stories about his grandfather's summer estate, a farm north of Tehran. Before the Islamic Revolution, his grandparents raised Caspian horses there, small mares that the children could ride. "One day, we will go back. The country will change. It must change," his father had said, but his father never got the chance to return home. Saman doubted he would either.

Taita Diego led the group inside the house. The Pomeranian puppies resumed barking and squeaking. The air-conditioning felt amazing. Saman had been so hot, standing under the afternoon sun by the pool. His stomach ached.

As they walked outside to their car, Taita Diego watched from the front door of the villa, his comedic smile replaced by closed lips. Saman waved to Taita Diego, but the tall man did not wave back. In his brown eyes, Saman saw a grim goodbye.

What is he thinking? Saman wondered. *Has he seen something else? Something he's left out?*

"I will see you tonight, at the grandmother ceremony." Maria told Thelma. "I'll text you what to wear, what to bring, and what to expect. You have enough time to get ready." She gave Thelma a hug.

"I don't know," Thelma said. "It's really soon. I haven't read much about ayahuasca."

"No time to wait," Maria said. "We won't have another grandmother ceremony for a few months, and there is a full moon tonight."

Sweat shimmered on Thelma's brow. *Or is it the Agua de Florida still on her skin?* Saman wondered. He felt dizzier now, or was he just tired? His head hurt. *I need to eat something as soon as we leave,* he thought.

Maria turned to him and raised her arms to embrace him. "And you, young man, take care of yourself until we meet again."

But before Saman could hug her, his legs snapped beneath him and his vision blurred. He gasped for air. Maria tried to catch him as he crumpled, but his weight knocked her to the ground. Thelma screamed.

In the distance, Saman heard Thelma shouting, "Oh my god! Call 911! Saman! Saman! Wake up!"

But he couldn't. Black nothingness encircled him and carried him away.

9

T helma flung open the car door, leaving Saman unconscious, face-up, sprawled out on her folded-down back seats. She ran inside the emergency room, screaming, "Help, help me."

A nurse rushed to her side. Breathless, they ran back to the car. Orderlies surrounded the vehicle and hoisted Saman out—one, two, three, and onto the stretcher, his legs limp and heavy. They strapped him in, his body present but his mind whisked away, gone. They pushed him up the ramp and into the hospital. Thelma ran inside, keeping behind the ER crew.

No, no, no, no.

Her purse smacked her back as it flapped behind her.

No. This isn't happening.

One door, another door, she heaved, her breath rapid, her eyes locked on the backs of the men pushing Saman on the moving mattress. The wheels of the stretcher clacked, metal on ceramic tiles. Faces turned in white gowns like ghosts, watching them as they ran down the hallway, and through the open doors of the Cleveland Clinic emergency room.

The nurse grabbed Thelma's shoulder to halt her. Saman's stretcher slipped behind the next door and then the next and then through two doors with glass windows. Thelma lost sight of them. She had tried to wake him up. She had screamed at him.

The nurse stepped in front of her, with one hand up, a crossing guard in a cotton scrub, and said, "Sorry Ma'am, I'm going to have to ask you to take a seat."

Thelma did not move; her focus fixed on the glass windows of the final ER door.

"Honey, come with me now." The nurse touched her shoulder and turned her like a child, leading her to the waiting area. She sat Thelma down in front of a cubicle.

The intake lady said, "I'm going to need to ask you a few questions, starting with the full name of the patient you came in with, and his date of birth and social security number, if you have it, and his insurance card or ID."

Thelma's shock shifted to overwhelm.

Saman is dying.

Facing the facts, she covered her eyes. Tears seeped between her fingers.

"It's okay," the woman said. "Take your time."

Thelma got up out of the chair, turned, and ran.

The nurse in turquoise scrubs caught her again, as she entered back into the hall of the emergency room.

"Ma'am, we need your cooperation here to get the details of your friend."

Thelma let the nurse hold her. She put her head in the nurse's frizzy, blond hair and sobbed, "I can't believe this is happening, you don't understand."

"Honey," The nurse rubbed her back. "Let's go to the

bathroom, get you cleaned up, and you can tell me what happened." She pulled a small tissue pack out of her scrub pocket and handed it to Thelma, leading her to the restroom.

"I don't know what's going to happen," Thelma sobbed as she splashed water on her face.

"Honey, no one does," the nurse said. "Is that fella you came in with your husband?"

Thelma shook her head, no. She glimpsed herself in the mirror, puffy, red eyes and mascara smeared on her cheeks.

"Boyfriend?"

Thelma nodded.

"Oh honey, I'm so sorry. What happened?"

Thelma stuttered, "He has—he has kidney failure." She wiped her eyes with a tissue to remove the black mascara smudges.

The nurse rubbed her back. "Well, he's in great hands now, so let's get you back to intake so we can figure out what the next step is and so you can get an update on your boyfriend."

Update on your boyfriend.

A sense of déjà vu jolted Thelma. She looked around. Everything felt strange. The hospital bathroom could have been in a hotel lobby, the brown tiles, the nurse's blond hair —she had heard and seen it all before. *But where?* In a dream? Thelma closed her eyes and took a deep breath. Her inner world flashed with the sight of Simon in the hospital bed from her dream.

Update on your boyfriend.

The nurse stared at her in the mirror, waiting.

Simon. Saman.

Thelma splashed water on her face once more. Taita Diego surfaced in her mind's eye. He wore a white scarf around his neck, embroidered with an orange tiger. Dancing in front of the fig tree from the cactus ceremony, he turned and pointed at the word, S I M O N.

Update on your boyfriend.

She saw herself walking down a long hospital hall. *Am I making this all up?* she thought. *Am I cracking up? Did grandfather scramble my brains like an egg?*

Taita Diego and Maria had helped lift Saman into the back of her car; there was no time to wait on an ambulance. She had begged them to come with her, to the hospital, to ride in the back with Saman, to hold him, to keep his body from moving, but they had refused. The shaman had another patient to see, and Maria had to leave to prepare for the evening ceremony. They had watched Thelma panicking, but they had not panicked. The shaman's face was as calm as the cats that observed them from the villa's front steps. Maria had tried to calm her.

"Be careful driving. Calm yourself down." Maria had warned. "Whatever happens to Saman is not in your control. Only driving as best you can is in your control."

But Thelma felt there was something she could do. There must be something.

The nurse stood with her at the sink. Other women came in and out of the bathroom stalls and washed their hands. The nurse waited for Thelma to open her eyes, but Thelma kept her head bowed. Water mingled with her tears and dripped from her chin. She pictured Saman in the hospital bed where Simon had been. In an instant, he was there. They interchanged. She saw the blond nurse smiling and fiddling with an IV bag. Thelma shuddered. The déjà vu did not wane. She gripped the edge of the sink, bracing her body against it. She wanted to scream.

"Come on." The nurse put another hand on her shoulder. "It's time to go now."

Thelma tensed every muscle in her body as if trying to draw up energy from a secret reservoir inside herself. She lifted her fingers off the sink and tightened her hands into fists.

Grandfather, grandmother, show me my path.

She opened her eyes and released her muscles.

As the nurse guided her out of the bathroom and back down the hall, a digital clock above the door to the emergency room displayed the time: 5:55 p.m.

TWO WOMEN with two small children, and a baby, rushed into the emergency waiting room. Without hesitation, Thelma knew the women must be Saman's sister and mother. Their thin noses, tan skin, angular jaws, and the way they moved together showed their lineage. She watched a live version of Saman's family photo album. His mother gathered the two children around her, a boy and a girl, maybe four and six. The woman Thelma imaged to be Saman's sister went to the intake desk. Thelma wondered if she should introduce herself.

The two children picked at each other and the younger boy whined for a snack from the hospital vending machine. Saman's mother scolded the boy in Farsi. She was stocky and in her sixties, wearing a maroon blouse and pressed black trousers with a patterned headscarf. Thick, black hair, free from any gray or trace of aging, peeked out of the scarf.

His mother has no idea I exist, Thelma thought, looking down at her clothes. She looked okay, but her face was a mess, not the best first impression. Would the intake nurse tell them who had brought in Saman? *Should I leave now?*

But she wanted to see Saman. No one had given her an update. Would they even update her, since she wasn't next of kin? She should have lied and said they were married.

I could still make it to the ceremony, Thelma thought. Would Saman want me to? Would he wake up and wonder where I was?

As Saman's sister turned back from the intake desk, her black-haired baby asleep in her arms, Thelma stood. Their eyes locked for a split second, and then the moment passed. Saman's sister took a seat next to her mother. The two women spoke in hushed tones, while the children tugged at their mother's clothes.

Grandmother will guide you, Maria had whispered to her.

Thelma left her chair and walked past Saman's family, unnoticed. She exited the hospital and drove straight to the nearest Wal-Mart. Grabbing a cart, she ran through the store, pulling what she needed from the shelves—a yoga mat, a hooded sweatshirt, water bottles, a bouquet of flowers, sweatpants, a blanket, and a pack of toilet paper rolls. She whipped past heavy-set black women, young Latino children, and wrinkled white men looking at fishing supplies until she reached the self-check-out line. She scanned her items, swiped her credit card, and ran back outside. Throwing the bags in the trunk, she got in the car and fastened her seat belt. As she steered south, the road was her only concern.

IN THE DIM light of the full moon, women and men encircled the fire, forming a tight loop. Despite rushing, Thelma was late. Everyone had already arrived. She worked her way around the clearing, looking for Maria, but did not see her. Trying to find a spot to squeeze her mat into proved difficult. People packed every part of the circle, some with umbrellas and inflatable mattresses, some meditating alone, some talking in hushed whispers to friends.

"Thelma," a woman's voice called her.

She turned to see Camilla, the yoga teacher, standing beside her, wide-eyed.

"I'm surprised to see you here. I didn't know you were coming tonight," Camilla said. She furrowed her brows. "Are you ok?"

"I'm glad to see you," Thelma breathed. Camilla was a welcome, familiar face on a day that felt more chaotic and more foreign with each passing hour.

"Here, come sit beside me, we can squeeze you in," Camilla said. She led Thelma to a spot facing the same fig tree where Thelma first saw Simon's name. Camilla motioned for the people beside her to push back so that Thelma could put her mat down.

As she spread her blanket, she realized she'd forgotten to buy a pillow. *Oh well.* She set out a roll of toilet paper and balled up her sweatshirt into a makeshift pillow. Claude smiled and waved to her from the alter.

Camilla leaned over and whispered, "How have you been?"

Before she could answer, Maria walked into the center circle, flanked by a shaman and two other men. Claude lit the fire, illuminating the shaman in orange branches of light. He was a wide, but short man and he wore a beaded necklace equal in size to Taita Diego's Jesus necklace, but with an orange-and-black, striped tiger.

"We will now open the ceremony and pray," the shaman said. "I use the Lord's Prayer, but you can pray to whoever you want to, the universe, Allah, Mickey Mouse, up to you." The crowd chuckled. He held his hands up and spoke.

"Our Father who art in heaven, hallowed be thy name. Thy kingdom come. Thy will be done."

Thelma closed her eyes. "Grandmother," she prayed, "please show me how I can help Saman. Please guide me grandmother. What do these messages mean?"

The shaman called each person to the altar to take the rapé tobacco. Thelma waited for her turn, her stomach already in knots.

Would Saman wake up? What had happened?

When she reached the altar, Maria stepped forward and embraced Thelma. They did not speak of Saman or the hospital. It was not the time.

The shaman stood on his tiptoes to reach Thelma's nose. She bent her knees a little to make it easier for him with her height. She braced herself for the burn of the rapé.

The shaman placed the double-headed pipe in one of her nostrils.

"Look in the eyes of the shaman, open your mouth, and exhale," Claude said.

In a puff of dust, the shaman blew rapé up her nose. She staggered back, then regained her composure and sat down. The tobacco burned her sinus cavities, and her attention focused on trying not to sneeze. She spat out the liquid as it dripped down the back of her throat.

I'm ready, grandmother. Guide me.

The shaman called each person up again, to drink the ayahuasca. He blessed them and his assistant poured each a small glass of brown liquid.

"Please receive your cup with a smile," the shaman said. "Beginning with a smile sets a positive tone for your journey."

The shaman's assistant motioned for Camilla to go up to the altar. Thelma would be next. Her pulse quickened. She knew much less about ayahuasca than the San Pedro cactus. What she did know was that ayahuasca caused some people to vomit violently, to feel burst apart, blasted to the stars, or to see hallucinations of snakes and jaguars.

Please go easy on me, Grandma.

The assistant motioned for her, and she walked to the altar. Taking the ayahuasca cup in both hands, she drank the brown liquid. It slid down her throat, a gritty thickness, almost the consistency of wet sand. It tasted like bitter, old wine. When she finished the cup, the assistant poured water into the same glass and swished it around with his finger to get all the ayahuasca sediment out. She drank from the glass again, then sat back down and glanced at Camilla. Camilla smiled and nodded in reassurance. Thelma waited. Nothing happened. The rest of the group finished receiving the medicine, and the shaman sang in Spanish.

Maybe I won't throw up, she thought.

Others in the circle staggered to 'wellness pits,' holes dug in the ground to collect vomit. As people came back from the pits, they walked choppy, like robots, or zombies. They struggled to pick up their feet and bent their arms at weird angles.

The ayahuasca shuffle, she thought.

Camilla got up, threw up, and returned to her mat.

Still nothing.

The shaman sang *icaros*, the ayahuasca songs from the Amazonian jungle, and played guitar. Thelma wished she could understand the lyrics. She caught a few words she recognized from the San Pedro ceremony—*pachamama,* which meant Mother Earth, and *curandero,* healer. The

shaman came and blew smoke on her from what looked like
an enormous Cuban cigar. Then he spat on the ground.

Everyone lay back on their mats, gazing up at the stars.
Thelma continued sitting up, watching the fire. An hour
passed. All she could think about was Saman in the hospital. She thought about sneaking out and checking her
phone. It was hard to keep her eyes open. She yawned.
Should I just go to sleep?

Lying down, she wrapped herself in the blanket. Saman
stayed in her mind, seeing his body collapsed on the pavement. Tears welled in her eyes and she cried into her sweat-
shirt-pillow.

Of course, the guy I like is dying, she thought. *I'm freaking
doomed.*

With this thought, nausea hit her like a hammer. She
bolted up and lurched forward, clutching her mouth with
her hand. *Oh, my god, I'm going to be sick.* She pushed herself
up and lunged toward the wellness pits, trying not to puke.

The three wellness pits looked like children's graves. Lit
candles inside mason jars illuminated the dirt trail to the
pits, but before she could reach the end of the path, sickness
washed over her. Like a trapped snake, her intestines
writhed and twisted. Acidic liquid shot up her esophagus.
She fell forward and grabbed a palm tree. As she clutched
its trunk, vomit spewed out of her mount and into the
brush. Her stomach convulsed and retched until nothing
came out but pockets of bitter bile that stung and burned
her throat. Sore and exhausted from dry heaving, she
doubled over, her mouth dripping with spit, eyes watering.
She gasped for air. Her legs weakened and wobbled. She
yearned for her mat, to lie down, but she could not move.
Like steel weights, her feet glued to the earth.

The night swam with patterns like insects, fireflies, thin

green snakes of light, electric geometric designs, and inter-secting triangles.

She felt a hand on her back. "Come with me," Maria said.

Crickets chirped and leaves rustled in the breeze. Dogs barked and bachata music pulsated low in the distance. The ayahuasca amplified the sounds of the farm. Her nausea subsided. The fire spat purple smoke. Prisms of color crackled around Maria like sparklers on the Fourth of July.

Thelma lay on her mat. Saman's presence radiated in the darkness, as if he slept beside her on the ground.

"Saman," she whispered, "please be ok."

Grandmother, guide me.

10

S aman opened his eyes. His sister Yalda leaned over him, scowling.

"Oh!" She jerked her head back. "You're awake?" She squinted at Saman.

He blinked. His vision was wet and blurry, like he was underwater. Machines beeped around him. The room stunk of cleaning products.

I'm in a hospital?

"Saman," his mother called him. "Saman jaan, can you hear me?"

He opened his eyes again. His mother and sister stood over him, looking down their long noses.

What happened to me?

"Ladies, please let him get some rest." Another voice in the room, rustling movements, white noise, breathing. His body was numb. He was so thirsty.

"Please," he whispered.

"He is awake." The voice of his sister.

"You gave us quite a scare." A brunette nurse, with a round, flabby face and cakey makeup stood beside him.

"Thirsty." Saman formed the word with chapped lips. His mouth hurt.

"That's a side-effect from the medication, honey," the nurse said, checking his temperature with a click of a small plastic gun that she held to his forehead. "I'll ask the doctor if you can have a wet sponge to suck on."

He fell back asleep. He woke up again with an alarm going off, a series of beeps repeating like a metronome.

I was with Thelma, he remembered.

A nurse adjusted buttons on a machine. She moved around, checking things. He tried to focus. He remembered the shaman, the pool, Maria. They had been leaving— where had they gone? Had they left? Where was Thelma?

Thelma.

"The girl I was with," he muttered. "Was there a girl with me?"

The nurse paused. "Your sister and your mother were here."

"No, a girl, a white girl."

"I haven't seen anyone, but I can check with the day nurse."

"Thelma," he said, "please see if she's here."

His throat burned. He tried to swallow. Pain cascaded down his chest. They must have intubated me, he thought.

What the hell had happened?

THE SKYLINE OF MIAMI, stacked with glass towers, hovered over the turquoise bay, shimmering like a mirage in the sun. The skyscrapers reflected and vibrated in the ocean's current. No clouds marked the azure sky. Barefoot in the grass, Thelma turned toward the water's edge. Saman stood by the shore, wearing a velvet tracksuit, the color of blueberries, with a silver reflective stripe down the side. With his long wavy hair pulled back in a ponytail, he was handsome. The light breeze blew tiny hairs around his face.

She had on a periwinkle dress with a white apron. *How odd,* she thought, *that I should be wearing this.*

Why am I dressed as Alice in Wonderland?

She held a large basket made of straw. It was heavy; she clutched it with both hands. *What was inside?* She tried to discern the contents. It contained fuzzy, brown rocks, or were they seeds?

She peered closer into the opening of the basket. *What were they?* She recoiled. The basket did not contain stones. It was full of dead bees. She gasped. Saman stepped closer to her and reached his hand in the basket. *No,* she thought, but she didn't speak. He fished deep into the lifeless pile of insects and pulled out a dead bee.

No, don't do that, she thought, frozen, aghast.

Saman raised the bee's body up between his two fingers. He cranked his arm back and launched the bee at the sun. Thelma pursed her lips together. *No, no, no.* She wanted to stop him. He picked up another bee from the basket and repeated the motion. *You can't do that,* Thelma thought.

"That won't work," she said.

Saman reached in again and pulled out a handful of the dead bees. He flung them one by one at the sun. They arched in the sky, then fell and disappeared. He threw them as if willing them to fly again.

"That won't work," Thelma repeated.

The bees dropped into the bay, each creating a tiny splash like a single teardrop.

My god, Thelma thought, suddenly self-aware. She knew this was a dream; she was lucid dreaming.

Saman threw more bees.

Grandmother, does this mean Saman is going to die? she asked. The idea made her heart race with fear.

No. Saman, no.

Thelma stared down into the basket, waiting for a reply.

A man said, "We're all going to die."

Thelma jerked up. Saman was gone. Simon stood in his place. He took the basket from her hands and held it up to her.

"Thelma, look inside," Simon whispered to her.

She looked inside the basket. The bees turned to water. Simon tilted the basket and poured it into the bay. She stared at Simon in shock. He set the basket down in the grass and embraced her.

"I love you," he whispered.

"I love you too," she replied, burying her head in his chest.

He glowed in the afternoon light.

"Simon," she said, "I missed you so much." At the sight of him, she knew it was true. She had missed him for a long, long time.

Simon wiped a tear from her cheek.

"Don't cry," he said.

He let go of her hand and dove into the bay. He disappeared.

Thelma ran to the shoreline.

"Simon, no!" Thelma screamed. She searched the sea for Simon. He was gone.

Grandmother why?

No answer.

The sun sat down behind the skyscrapers; the moon rose over the waves. Thelma gazed at her reflection in the water. Her body transformed. She was not a girl anymore.

She became a gray wolf, an oscillating, pale, canine shape in the moonlight. The wolf rested on its haunches. It leaned its head forward and drank from the bay. The Miami buildings turned into mountains, the ocean a dark blue lake. Snow blanketed the green grass. She stretched her front legs out and ran away, through the cold night, over hills and icy pastures, through fields streaked with unknown songs that she did not hear, but saw.

She crossed a chasm of time and returned to the warm, fire-filled grandmother medicine circle.

THE NURSE BROUGHT Saman his phone in a plastic bag.

"We found this in your pants pocket," she said. "You did come in with a girl. She stayed for a while then left. That's what the intake nurse remembered, a tall, blonde girl."

Saman took the phone.

"Try to get some rest. The doctor will talk to you in the morning." The nurse adjusted one of his machines. "Good-night now." She switched off the light.

Saman lifted his hand. In the dim, green glow of the heart monitor, he examined the bandages covering his arm. *Did they change my fistula?* he wondered. *Did I get dialysis last night? Or is it tonight?* He tried not to move too much. *How long have I been here?* His throat still ached, and his legs were stiff. His back itched.

He lifted his arm as best he could so he could see the screen of his cell phone. He attempted to unlock it. His movements felt mushy, like he was sinking in gravy. *The meds*, he thought, *they've drugged me.* He tried again. The phone clicked open. He called Thelma.

No answer.

He redialed her number.

No answer.

And again. And again.

She's gone. No wonder. He put the phone beside him.

He wanted to give up.

THE VISION WAS OVER; Thelma lay next to Camilla. The shaman sang over her, shaking a rattle. Maria fanned smoke from an iron skillet full of ashes. Thelma curled into a fetal position and tucked the blanket over her head, praying for grandmother to let her sleep.

THE LIGHTS WOKE SAMAN UP. The night nurse moved around the bed. Bag check. Monitor check. Temperature check. Catheter check. Lights off again. Saman picked up his phone and tried Thelma. No response. No dial tone. Her phone now was off. He sank back to sleep like a stone hurled into the sea.

DAWN OOZED through Thelma's flannel blanket. Roosters crowed. Dewdrops littered the grass with tiny pearls of water. The shaman's assistant pulled her up and led her to the altar. In a daze, she leaned on his shoulder, hardly able to stand, half-asleep. Claude turned her palms face up, moving her like she was a mannequin. He stretched her arms forward to receive the shaman's final blessing.

THE DOCTOR WHEELED his stool beside Saman and flipped through his chart. Saman's mother and sister watched from the back of the room, waiting. Yalda's husband had taken the kids home so Yalda could stay with her mother and Saman.

"So, the good news is that your potassium levels are responding to the medication," the doctor said. He scooted closer to Saman. "But unfortunately, we need to keep you here to make sure all your levels are stable. You had a pretty significant collapse. Your blood pressure was very high, which puts you at risk for a stroke. Your nephrologist will be in shortly to discuss your treatment options."

"What does that mean?" Saman's mother asked in her thick Persian accent.

The doctor glanced at Saman's mother. "As to how this will impact his overall prognosis, I think it's best the nephrologist explains in more detail."

"Can this get him moved up on the transplant list?" Saman's sister asked.

"Again, a question for the nephrologist." The doctor stood up.

Saman already knew what it all meant. He had read the studies and looked at the statistics. Most people with his condition did not last more than five or six years before their hearts or lungs started to fail. It was only a matter of time before he had a stroke or an aneurysm, cardiac arrest or worse. His mother and sister knew his situation was grim, but they did not accept the truth. In their mind, he was the small percentage that survived. They failed to consider that he might be in the majority. Without his kidneys regulating his body, no hospital or dialysis machine could keep all his organs working forever. It could be in ten months or ten minutes, but unless he found a compatible kidney donor, he would die.

THELMA MADE her way to the bathroom. Looking in the mirror, she felt electrified, as if the ayahuasca had injected steroids into her muscles. The weight of her sadness lifted, and the dawn brought her conviction. She knew what she had to do.

Rolling up her mat and blanket, she left the circle before breakfast began.

Camilla followed her out to her car. "You should stay for the integration. You need to eat something and rest. The medicine could still be working in your system. It's not safe to drive."

Thelma kept walking.

"I'm getting Maria, I don't think you should go," Camilla said, following her.

"I'll be fine. I need to go." Thelma got in her car.

The morning sun streamed in sideways through the field by the farm. Her phone was dead. She plugged it into the car charger and backed onto the road. Flying past acres of fruit trees, tall queen palms, gas stations, and Seminole Indian casinos, she made her way back to the hospital, parked, and went inside to find Saman.

Grandmother, please let him be alive.

YALDA SAT on the edge of the hospital bed. "I have to go home and relieve Amir; he can't handle the kids alone for too long."

"It's fine." Saman said.

His sister crinkled her forehead. "You will be okay with Mom here?"

"Of course!" Saman's mother barked from the armchair in the corner, trying to figure out the hospital's TV remote control.

"Take Mom with you," he said. He wanted them all to leave.

"At least you have your own room," Yalda said. "I'll come back later with the kids to check on you."

"No, please don't, you'll get them all sick from the hospital germs. Really, I'm fine."

"Okay, and I'm calling the mosque to see if they can put out a broadcast to find a donor," Yalda said.

Saman did not bother to tell her it wouldn't work. Since his father had died, his sister and mother had prayed at the mosque every Friday, but what good had it done? He had stopped believing in Islam as soon as he could read. Why would anyone at the mosque help? He never went there, and no one knew him. If his own sister was not ready to give him her kidney, why would a stranger?

Yalda kept talking. "And I'm going to speak to my friend, Gohar—she has a cousin in Tehran who bought a kidney."

"Just please, can you go by my house and feed StanGetz? My keys should be in my pants pockets."

His sister hesitated. "What do I feed him?"

Saman sighed. "The cat food in the bottom of the fridge. Just fill his bowl and make sure he has water."

She nodded. "Ok but you owe me."

"I'll owe you my whole life, which will be over soon," Saman said.

"Stop being morbid. Okay Mom, bye." Yalda waived at her mother but received only a grunt in response. Their mother had gotten the TV turned on and was channel surfing.

"Nothing but Mexican shows," she mumbled.

Yalda left. Saman tried to sleep, but only a few minutes passed before the door opened again and Yalda came back inside.

"You forget something?" His mother looked over from the TV.

"Um, Saman, there is a girl here to see you." Yalda raised her eyebrows.

"A girl?" Saman's mother dropped the remote.

Thelma entered the hospital room. Everyone went quiet. Pieces of grass stuck to Thelma's t-shirt and her uncombed hair hung loose and oily around her face. She smelled like burnt wood, but her eyes danced with energy, almost with madness.

Thelma rushed up to Saman.

"Saman, oh my god, I'm so glad you are alive." She clutched his hand in hers.

Saman's mother gasped. Yalda stood in the doorway, mouth agape, waiting for an explanation.

"I didn't know what to do, I thought you were dead," Thelma said, her eyes searching his for answers.

Saman's eyes watered. "I thought you had just bounced. I couldn't remember what happened. I tried to call you and your phone was off."

"I ran out of battery. I didn't want to leave you but, your family came and I thought I should go." She glanced at

Saman's mother and smiled, then turned back to Saman. "I went to the ceremony."

He wanted to sit up, but he couldn't. "Oh my god, the ceremony. I remember now. I forgot."

She nodded.

Saman's mother stood up and moved toward Thelma. "Excuse me, who are you? I don't believe we've met," his mother said.

Thelma jerked up and stuck out her hand. "I'm so sorry, I'm Thelma."

Saman's mother hesitated and looked at Saman.

"She's my girlfriend, Mom. Sorry, I was going to introduce you, but I didn't have a chance," he lied.

"I see," Saman's mother said. With reservation, she shook Thelma's hand.

"Can you guys give us a minute please?" Saman asked.

No one moved.

"Yalda, please take Mom to the gift shop or something."

Yalda snapped to attention and ushered her mother out of the room, shooting back a surprised look at Saman and mouthing, *What the fuck?*

After they left, Saman turned to Thelma. "Sorry my mom is old-fashioned. She thinks Persians should only date other Persians so they can make Persian babies or else all the Persians will die out." He wanted to laugh, but it hurt his stomach.

Thelma sat down on the doctor's stool. "What happened?"

"It's really complicated, but basically my kidneys are messing up my heart."

Thelma kissed him on the lips. "Are you going to be okay?"

He tried not to cry. "I could use a kidney transplant."

One tear slid out and rolled to the side of his face and into his hair.

Thelma held his hand. "You're going to be fine, I know you will."

"I'm like an ecosystem. When one thing goes wrong, everything gets out of balance. My condition is like flowers sprayed with pesticides—then bees get poisoned from the flowers and die. Without the bees, the other plants don't get pollinated. Things that eat the plants don't have enough food. It's a chain reaction until something major gets messed up and the whole system collapses."

"The bees are not going to die," Thelma replied through gritted teeth.

"I mean they are basically already dead. I can't sugar-coat this situation anymore."

"No." She shook her head with force, shaking her hair. "No. Grandmother showed me what to do."

"Grandmother? What did you see at the ceremony?"

She nodded and pressed his hand. "I will get you a new kidney," she said. "I'll fly to New York and convince Simon's daughter to give you Simon's kidney."

Saman blinked. *What?* Her expression was ferocious.

Thelma slipped off her bracelet from the first ceremony.

"Here," she said. "Wear this, so you can't die while I'm gone, because you have to give me my bracelet back."

"Thelma, don't say that."

"Just do it." She fastened the bracelet onto his wrist, kissed him goodbye, and left.

He did not ask how she would do it, or how she knew Simon's kidney would be a match. The determination in her eyes left him with no doubt that she would try as hard as she could.

For the first time in a long time, Saman felt hope.

AT A GALLOP, Thelma reached the end of the hallway and spotted Saman's sister and mother. She ran to them. They stopped, startled.

"Listen," Thelma said, "I think I found a donor for Saman. I want to get your number, in case I need any information to verify the match."

Yalda scrunched her face. "A match? From who?"

"Someone I know. I've got to go now, but I will call you and explain."

"Give her your number," Saman's mother nudged Yalda.

Yalda looked Thelma up and down, then pulled a piece of grass off Thelma's shirt.

"Forgive me for my concern," Yalda said in a condescending tone, "but I've never heard Saman mention anything about you and then you just came in and . . ." She trailed off.

Thelma frowned. She had no patience for disbelief. She needed to get to New York before she lost her nerve.

"Well then, it was nice to meet you," she said and walked around them, heading for the exit.

"Wait, okay here." Yalda held out her phone, but Thelma was already across the lobby. She did not turn back. She would go home, take a shower, find a flight to New York, and leave today. Her plan had to work. Rushing out of the Cleveland Clinic's revolving doors, she ran through the expansive parking lot to her car.

HOME, inside her apartment, Thelma opened her computer's search engine. If she left soon, she could be in New York that night. She booked the flight and pulled a suitcase out of the top of her closet.

November, New York, it will be cold, she thought.

She slid a plastic tub out from under her bed and grabbed her winter jacket and a pair of ankle boots. It would likely take more than a day to convince Simon's daughter, Raquel to explain the whole story, but she eventually would. She had to. Grandmother had shown her in the vision by switching Simon to Saman. It would work.

She glanced at the clock on her phone. II:II. *Why did all these repeat numbers keep appearing in her life? 5:55, I:II?* She saw 3:33 too the other day. *What did it all mean?* Her flight boarded in four hours, still time to take a shower. The hot water melted over her like a chocolate sundae. Lathering her hair with shampoo, her frantic pace began to slow. Switching off the water and stepping out of the shower, she dried herself and took a deep breath. She was ready to see Simon, for the first time in fifteen years.

Wrapping a towel around her torso, she picked up her cell phone. There was a notification, a Facebook message. She opened the phone.

Thank you for the flowers. That was very kind. I wanted to let you know that I am sorry to say, my father has passed away. He left us on November 21st. Memorial service details can be found here: http://www. danielsfuneralhome.com/SimonAmalfitano

- Love Raquel

Thelma stared at the screen in disbelief. She dropped to her knees and shrieked.

11

On the cold tile floor, Thelma woke up shivering. In the dark, she crawled on her hands and knees, her towel slipping off her body. Naked, with wet hair, the wolf from her vision returned to her. With one thought came many. She replayed the scene at the bay — Simon, his smile, the love in his eyes.

How long have I been asleep?

She pulled herself to the edge of her sofa and prayed.

"Grandmother, grandfather, please show me the way."

She breathed in, filling her lungs, held her breath then exhaled.

"Grandmother and grandfather, all the magic you have shown me, what does it mean? I need clarity. Help me. Help Saman. Don't let him die."

She waited for an answer, a word, a sign. Nothing came. Her mind stayed still, like the air of the room, blank space.

She turned her back to the sofa and slumped down, splaying her feet in a V-shape on the floor under the coffee table.

How am I going to tell Saman?

What will I even say? She had seen the hope in his eyes. He believed her visions; he believed in the medicine's power, a force beyond the human grasp.

"Please, grandmother," she whispered again. Was she calling on her ancestors, or a plant, or a God? She did not know but believed that if she called, something would answer. She concentrated all her force and will on her questions. Still, no response came.

An hour passed, and she gave up; cold, she put on a robe.

As she stood by the window, looking out at the Intracoastal, the night's clouds covered any sight of stars. No ship traffic, or cars. It must be three or four in the morning, she realized.

She found her phone. The message from Raquel was still there.

He left us . . .

Thelma leaned her forehead against the glass window, welcoming back tears. *Tears for Simon*, she thought, for the love I wanted from him, but never really got to have.

She closed her eyes. *What had Simon said to her on the shore?* She tried to remember his words before he jumped into the sea.

The sea. Had he said, "see inside?" *The Sea Inside*, wasn't that the name of a film? She shook her head and looked deeper into the darkness of her own mind.

Look inside. He had said, "Look inside."

Wandering into her bedroom, she opened her closet bifold doors and pushed her sundresses out of the way. She reached into the corner, up against the wall, and with some difficulty, dragged out an old, wooden jewelry armoire, the size of a filing cabinet. The armoire was heavy and hard to move. She scraped it across the tile floor to the middle of the room and plopped down in front of it. The wood cabinet was chipped, the stain peeling in places. The armoire belonged to her mother's mother, who she had never met. Her mother had passed it down to her, as a Christmas gift.

As a young girl, the box held trinkets and pins from trips, magnets from Disney World, and mood rings. As she got older, love letters and condoms filled the armoire, Polaroids of herself as a teenager, and now anything of great significance she tucked into the drawers, from her social security card to her first digital camera.

Thelma took a deep breath, then wiggled out the bottom sections of the chest. Photographs lined the green-velvet drawer. She carried it to her bed and lay beside it, pulling out each picture one by one, like a child picking petals off a daisy, until she found the photo she wanted to hold.

There was Simon, printed on Kodak paper; he sat next to her on a sofa, wearing a blue suit and a black shirt, unbuttoned at the collar. They were in a nightclub, on New Year's Eve in Paris. She wore a sequined, gold slip dress that hung off her shoulders with spaghetti straps, curving down to reveal the skin between her small breasts. They clasped their hands together, smiling at each other. Around them, people laughed, and confetti flew in the air, women in skimpy outfits kissed their boyfriends, but Thelma and Simon, transfixed on the couch, gazed into each other's eyes, mad with love, oblivious to the world. In that moment, they experienced love in the present tense. They had not noticed the professional photographer taking their picture. As they left, arm in arm, the sun beginning to rise over the city's cobblestone streets; they saw photos laid out by the exit, displayed for sale. Simon insisted on buying theirs. He bought two copies, one for her and one for him.

Where was his photo now?

She pressed hers to her chest.

"Goodbye Simon, my love, goodbye," she said.

She took the photograph to the living room. Taking one of her pictures of the ocean off the wall, she removed it from the frame and inserted the photo of her and Simon.

Look inside, she thought.

She rehung the frame. "I won't forget you Simon, my love, not this time."

Thelma turned on all the lights and got out her camera. She had not yet looked at the pictures of Saman at the river.

"Please let them be good," she whispered, and stuck the camera's memory card into the computer.

And they were good. More than good, the photos were breathtaking. The daylight was right, the look in his eyes— overpowering and true. In the most powerful image, Saman held out his arms like a cross. The water gleamed; his hair blew in the breeze. Golden sunlight and feathers fell around him, midair, bright patches of color, soft in the slow-moving stream, the foliage a dazzling bouquet of greens and yellows with glimpses of blue sky. She made a few adjustments to the image, the contrast and the exposure. She warmed up the photo until he radiated with orange light, a phoenix transforming into a man.

Outside her window, the morning sun cracked over the Intracoastal like an egg. The waters brightened from black to indigo. Thelma finished the photograph and began to type.

Have you ever lost a love?

Have you ever felt your heart break?

Have you ever wondered when you would experience love again, or if you ever would?

I have.

You feel alone and adrift, you can't find your way, like you've gotten off track.

You've lost the path in the woods and there are no breadcrumbs for you to trace your way back.

You look at everyone you meet and wonder if they have the answers.

Or are you the only one struggling?

Well, I have found love again, and I don't want to lose it this time.

The man in this photo is named Saman, and I love him, but he is dying and he's dying fast.

He needs a kidney, or else our love cannot last.

Please help us, she typed.

Please don't let our love die. If you would like to help us by donating a kidney, or if you know someone who could be a donor, please contact us as soon as you can.

She read over the passage a few times, then added her phone number.

Using the photo and the text, she began to post, to print, to email and comment and tag. She gathered up a stack of the printed flyers, and a roll of tape, got dressed and left her apartment to canvas the town, the county, the state if it came to that. She would find Saman a kidney. She would keep her promise.

12

Strings of carnations and balloons hung from the gate of *La Tierra de Deseos,* the Land of Wishes. Guests parked on the banks of the banana farm in every direction, wearing all-white, per Thelma's instructions. A campfire glowed in the middle of the clearing. Maria gathered the colorful bouquets of roses and lilies and sunflowers that each visitor brought. She placed them on the altar, preparing for the ceremony. On a table covered with lace cloth, Claud placed candles, crystals, and a photo of Thelma and Saman, arms around each other at the beach.

Some thought they were crazy to hold the ceremony before his transplant, but Saman knew a lot crazier things were possible. In fact, crazy things happened every day, if you believed in them.

Next to Thelma's father, Saman waited. He adjusted a lei of plumeria around his neck. He wore white pants and a simple, linen short-sleeved shirt. Camilla, Maria, and Yalda watched from the circle with Saman and Thelma's mothers and the rest of their guests. Reams of translucent, silver, and green chiffon spiraled around the clearing, sprinkled with flower petals. Thelma's camera assistant, Carlos, snapped photos. Claude made a heart of red roses and rocks around the fire in the center of the circle.

In the back-garden, where Saman and Thelma had first met, Thelma waited, in her white dress, with her grandmother and grandfather, one from her mother's side and one from her father's, her last living grandparents. They would usher her down the path and reveal her to Saman.

On the other side of his mother sat another woman, Rita Cando. Rita beamed at him and waved. He waved back. His mother believed it was a miracle from Allah that Rita Cando had come into their lives, but Saman knew it was all because of Thelma. Her story and the photograph of Saman had circulated far and wide, across the web and onto people's cellphones and televisions, broadcast on morning shows and evening news channels. Most people wanted to help, but could not donate their organs. A group online started a campaign, using Thelma's post to raise funds to assist with the transplant, for whenever they found a donor. In one day, they gathered over $400,000 dollars.

Within a week, a friend of Maria's named Rita, living in Orlando, wrote to them. She had seen the picture and read Thelma's text. Rita, having lost her own husband to pancreatic cancer, felt a kinship with Thelma. Saman reminded her of her husband when he was young. Widowed and alone, with no children of her own, she wanted to help.

Maria assisted and they brought Rita to Miami to test her to see if she would be an eligible donor. The pair matched. Thelma and Saman would use some of the money for the transplant procedure, and the rest they used to pay off the mortgage on Rita's house, a thank you for donating her precious organ.

With the kidney transplant lined up, Saman took Thelma to the beach where they'd first kissed.

He knelt down in the sand. "You asked grandfather medicine to show you your true path, then you almost ran into me on the path on your way back from the bathroom," he laughed. "Now I want to ask you to walk this path with me called life. Thelma Chenoweth, will you be my wife?"

She had cried when he pulled out the engagement ring and slipped it onto her finger, a gold band with a diamond in the center, surrounded by two green emeralds. On the inside, he'd engraved 11/11, the date of the morning they met.

He still wore her beaded bracelet from the first ceremony on one wrist, and his bracelet on the other, a reminder to take care of himself, to eat, to follow the doctor's orders, to keep living every day, so he could stay on this planet with her.

Saman took a deep breath.

Taita Diego strummed an acoustic guitar. His assistant played a flute and Maria sang,

> *Flower of water, where do you come*
> *from, where are you going?*
> *I searched the universe and found the love*
> *of another.*
> *In the heart of my heart*
> *She bore this earth and truth*
> *This deep and profound secret,*
> *The care and love of another.*

Thelma emerged from the tall trees. She wound down the spiral path, into the clearing, white sundress swishing. Green leaves dappled with red rosebuds crowned her blond hair. Leaning on a mahogany cane, her grandfather held her left arm. Her grandmother smiled beside her, their right arms linked.

Step by step, the three walked the inner edge of the circle, until they reached Saman, and he took Thelma by the hand.

MUSHROOM HONEYMOON CHAPTER ONE EXCERPT

A SNEAK PEAK AT BOOK TWO IN THE PSYCHEDELIC LOVE SERIES

Saman lingered on the sidewalk in front of the dialysis center. The yellow, single-story cement structure looked small, like he'd already outgrown it. Storm clouds brewed behind the building, turning the sky dark gray. *I should feel relieved*, he thought, but instead, he felt something else. He took a deep breath and got in his car.

Skipping the highway, he navigated northwest in silence, to their new home in Fort Lauderdale. Fat drops of rain smacked against the windshield and thunder boomed in the distance. The drive felt somber, not like an accomplishment, but like a departure. *So much is about to change.* He wouldn't need dialysis after the transplant, but he'd be immunocompromised. Transplant patients had to take immunosuppressants for the rest of their lives, to keep their new kidney from being attacked as a foreign invader.

Stopping at a red light, something his mother said earlier that week lingered in his mind like dust on a shelf. "Now you can leave that awful dialysis place behind, with all those poor people, and focus on moving up at the radio station."

The comment bothered him — first, because his mother thought the center was awful; second, because he never defined the other patients as "poor people"; and third, because his mother had never suggested that he try for a promotion at the radio station.

The light turned green. Had his mother expected him to die? He frowned. But what did she expect now? There weren't any better positions for him at the station. He crawled behind a line of cars to the next stoplight. *I should have taken the highway*, he thought.

The downpour increased in intensity. A disheveled, deeply tanned, older man carrying a black umbrella and a bucket full of roses walked between the stopped vehicles. *He shouldn't be out in this storm*. Whenever it rained in Florida, lightning followed.

The man held a clump of red roses covered in clear plastic. Saman made eye contact, to show respect, but shook his head, "no."

"For your wife," the man yelled.

Thunder cracked overhead. The rose dealer rapped on the window with his knuckle. "Ten dollars for two?"

I could get one for Rita and one for Maria, Saman thought. He'd see both of them that afternoon for a private magic mushroom ceremony, a gift from Maria to him and Rita before the special day of the kidney operation. The flowers would be a nice gift and something to adorn the ceremony's altar. He fished out his wallet from his back pocket. The only thing inside was a fifty-dollar bill. Saman cracked the window. "Do you have change?"

"Yes. I have." The man passed two red roses to Saman.

"I'll take white ones, please," Saman said.

The man swapped the flowers and handed him the

white roses. Saman gave the man his fifty-dollar bill and the man bolted across the street with the cash.

"Hey, wait, my change!" Saman yelled.

The running man did not look back.

Saman scowled. Then again, it was pouring rain; maybe he would have done the same if he was desperate enough to sell roses in a thunderstorm? But Saman wasn't in a financial position to hand out fifty-dollar bills. Between paying off the mortgage on Rita's house, a gift to thank her for donating her kidney, and the purchase of their own house, he'd be in debt forever.

The man sat at the covered bus stop across the street, acting as if nothing had happened.

The stoplight turned green, and lightning cracked overhead. In his side mirror, Saman caught the man walking to the other side of the street, to target the next round of cars. *I guess he needs the money more than I do.* Saman glanced at the roses. The flowers weren't worth fifty dollars, but Rita and Maria would like them.

He switched on a bluegrass band called *Doggy Bowl*, and tapped the steering wheel in rhythm with the drums, singing along.

> *"Hammer girl, hammer down the house.*
> *Gonna tear these old walls out and make*
>   *something else."*

As he drove, Saman concentrated on the mushroom ceremony. Maria advised setting an intention before eating the sacred fungi. *I could focus on finding the right next step in my life*, he thought. Though it was hard to see beyond the transplant, and his recovery could take six, even eight weeks.

"Just get me through this alive," he murmured, and turned up the volume on his music, louder and louder, until it blocked the roar of the storm outside.

ACKNOWLEDGMENTS

Special thanks to Stephane Poirier for inspiring elements in this book and for sharing your story with me. Thank you to Agah, for letting me audition my ideas and for being my biggest supporter.

Special thanks as well to my mother, Carol and to Amy Burrows and Rachel Schleisman Fosness for your support and feedback. Thank you Carlos, Gloria, Monica, and Kyle for sharing what you share with the world. Thank you Dylan Garity for your editing work. Thank you Fred and Max for helping me decide on a name and cover design. Thank you to Jeanine Eliz and Louis Nathaniel Cinelli for bringing this story to life in picture form. Thank you Deanna Lambert for always being my sounding board and creative wonder woman. Thank you Mandi Gray for being my fellow word-count witch. Thank you Heather Knorr for your language and Spanish revision help.

Thank you most to my readers, and special thanks to my beta readers and launch team. Love you all! XXXOOO

THANK YOU

If you enjoyed this book, or if you hated it — I would love to hear your feedback.

Please consider leaving a review on the platform where you purchased this book.

Follow my author page on Amazon:
amazon.com/author/charlottedune

Email me, or subscribe to my newsletter and get a gift from me here:
http://charlottedune.com/contact/

ABOUT THE AUTHOR

Charlotte Dune is a romance, travel, and adventure writer based in South Florida. Her writing explores self-discovery, love, and exotic locations. She has a passion for travel, reading, nature, and expanding consciousness with entheogenic practices.

When not writing, you will find her by the pool with her partner, daughter, and their Schnauzer, Morkie, and extra-large cat.

www.charlottedune.com

facebook.com/CharlotteKDune

twitter.com/charlotte_dune

instagram.com/charlottedune

amazon.com/author/charlottedune

goodreads.com/charlottedune

Made in the USA
Columbia, SC
23 May 2021